Moonlit Match

Cauldron Falls, Volume 6

Solara Gordon

Published by THE EARTH MOVED, LLC, 2024.

This is a work of fiction. Similarities to real people, places, or events are entirely coincidental.

MOONLIT MATCH

First edition. October 6, 2024.

Copyright © 2024 Solara Gordon.

ISBN: 979-8988654988

Written by Solara Gordon.

Also by Solara Gordon

Cascade Bay
Love Reborn
Reunited By Choice
Love's Triple Play
Three Hearts In Love
For the Love of Three

Cauldron Falls
Believe In Love
Home for the Holidays
Three Hearts Entwined
A Mate of Their Own
Moonlit Match
A Christmas Reunion

Peyton Corners
Falling for You
Caught by Love's Slow Burn

Standalone
A Heart's Desire
To Love You Again
To Love You Again

Watch for more at https://solaragordon.com/.

WELCOME INTRODUCTION

Welcome to Cauldron Falls, where full moon matches and Sadie Hawkins dances ignite sparks and join hearts as the magic of love fills the air. Cauldron Falls citizens blend human, supernatural, and magics together as full moon sparks and love magic mix.

Polyamorous/Menage matches (triads and/or quads) and dyadic pair bondings are happening. Each story brings a unique love magic and full moon spark blending to life.

Moonlit Match is Agatha Clemons, and Peter Drake's blue full moon Halloween Sadie Hawkins match story. A witch matchmaker's carefully guarded secret is at risk when a mysterious shapeshifter with his own hidden past moves to Cauldron Falls, turning her world upside down and unraveling everything she's worked to protect.

Below is a list of each book in the Cauldron Falls series with a books2read link. I hope you enjoy immersing yourself in each Cauldron Falls story. Stay tuned for more from Cauldron Falls, the spin-off series about Cauldron Falls' sister city, Sylvan Valley and Sylvan Valley Cauldron Falls founding families' stories.

A Christmas Reunion: books2read.com/u/baB5Aq[1]
A Mate of Their Own: books2read.com/u/4E9oJz[2]
Believe In Love: books2read.com/u/m2QWer[3]
Three Hearts Entwined: books2read.com/u/3y28qe[4]
Home for the Holidays: books2read.com/u/496OAY[5]

---

1. https://books2read.com/u/baB5Aq
2. https://books2read.com/u/4E9oJz
3. https://books2read.com/u/m2QWer
4. https://books2read.com/u/3y28qe
5. https://books2read.com/u/496OAY

CHAPTER ONE

Welcome to Cauldron Falls

Monday Afternoon

Peter Drake slowed as he came to the end of the highway exit ramp. The roadside signs read, 'Welcome to Cauldron-Sylvan County' and 'Cauldron Falls-35 Miles'. He picked up speed as he turned onto the two-lane road. The dashboard navigation showed similar roads. Rural spaces. Farmland and woods until he reached Cauldron Falls, nestled close to Sylvan Mountain.

Peter opened the driver and passenger windows. Air rushed into the car, washing over him, blowing any remaining large city smells off him. He inhaled deeply. Scents rushed up his nostrils. Wet earth. Crumbling fallen leaves. Clean air. No lingering car fumes or heavy pollution. He could easily make out the peak of Sylvan Mountain and the rest of the mountains surrounding Cauldron Falls' sister city, Sylvan Valley.

Moving cross country hadn't turned out as simple as he planned. Starting over meant change. Change that ignited other changes. Figuring out priorities, making decisions, crossing things off to-do lists and surprises. MacGruder's restaurant had become available during one of his visits. Buying the restaurant and continuing the remodeling, the prior owner had started placed more surprises and items on his Cauldron Falls to-do list.

He'd had enough additional surprises. Four-hour flight. Three-hour drive. The final stretch was thirty more minutes of driving. Thirty more minutes until he reached his new home. The movers were due Friday, midday. The builder's final walk-through video showed off light-colored walls, hardwood floors, dusty blue carpeted bedrooms, and walk-in closets. The master bath and hall bath mirrored the color scheme throughout the rest of the house. A peaceful, outdoorsy feeling drawing the occupants in. Inviting them to relax in the ambiance called home. Home to a shapeshifter who spent too many years in California moving up and down the coast as his job and company necessitated.

His cell phone rang as he slowed for a stop light. Caller ID displayed his cousin Carlos's phone number. Peter closed the windows and tapped the talk button. "Hey, Carlos."

"About time you answered."

"You could've left a message. I checked voice mail before I left the airport and the car dealership."

Carlos's chuckle boomed out of the speaker. "Teasing cousin. Glad you're on your way."

"Almost there. On Route Forty-Three. Not much traffic. You at your place or the house?"

"Ingrid is making up a shopping list. We set up some extra furniture we had at your place." Carlos's wife spoke in the background. "You going to the house or coming here? I'm heading to the market and running errands."

"There for now. We can check out the house tomorrow. Ask Ingrid if mutton stew makings are on the list."

Carlos's voice muffled. Peter made out a word or two. No hot sauce or cabbage. Baked from scratch yeast rolls and homemade ice cream. Ingrid enjoyed cooking and preparing family meals.

"Okay, mutton stew ingredients are on the list. You're in luck on the rolls and ice cream."

"Caught that part of the conversation. Just passed a sign saying Cauldron Falls twenty-five miles."

"See you in twenty to thirty minutes. Ingrid says we gotta help unload the car when she gets back."

Peter chuckled. "Pitching in gets the stew cooking that much faster. See you soon."

Peter ended the call, reopened the windows and tuned in the local yatch rock music station. Oldies and soft rock flowed out of the speakers.

Inheriting the last unclaimed acre of his great-grandfather's original farmland presented the chance he'd been looking for. Build his own place. A place he could call home. Home that met his needs. His wants and desires. Enough wooded area surrounded the perimeter boundaries. He wasn't worried about his neighbors seeing him returning from full moon shifting. Almost getting caught streaking through part of a couple of San Diego and Los Angeles parks after the moon set was something he wasn't about to repeat. City-dwelling shapeshifting packs were officially on their own. His resignation caught the Southern California chapter of the Supernatural, Humans and Magics Council off guard. National organization hounded him for three months about his decision. SH&M could do their spying and investigating on their own. It was time the Great Reveal by-laws were updated. Council business, not his.

Few knew all his reasons for leaving California. Starting over and changing how he approached life. Too many years hiding his true nature. Too many moments when attraction felt right and revealing his duality failed. Women who seemed like a good fit. Attraction and chemistry were there. Fleeting more than a steadfast pulsation.

Peter let out a deep sigh. He was rural and there was no way around it. Moonlight and full moons drew him. Brought him comfort and peace. Peace of mind and tranquility deep inside for both him and his wolf. He glanced in the rearview mirror. No one behind him. Side mirrors confirmed the same.

Peter opened the sunroof, tossed back his head and let go a long, low howl. The first in two months. Praise Lupa, he could morph at will. The one genetic trait he thanked his Brindle Wolf relatives and heritage for. It felt good to let his inner angst and frustrations out. He howled a bit louder and longer. Keeping his growing ire intact had taken both him and his wolf watching, waiting, and watching more.

Carlos's invitation to stay with Ingrid and him until the house was finished and the movers unpacked their truck moved up his leaving by two weeks. A week closing on the sale of his Los Angeles home and prepping travel plans. Early Midwest fall weather had delayed his car delivery. He'd spent three days visiting with his sister and niece until his car arrived at the dealership this morning. Catching up with his one close sibling empowered him. Empowered him in ways he'd forgotten. Blood family and family of choice. His family of choice helped him pack, sort through things and wished him well in the next phase of his life journey. A few accepted invitations for the human holiday celebrations, Thanksgiving and Christmas. Halloween was for his supernatural blood family and the few magics and human friends he'd made on his trips to get his starting over conceptualized, started, and now in the home stretch.

Peter grinned as he passed the next road sign. Cauldron Falls fifteen miles. He glanced at the speedometer. Sixty-five in a forty-five-speed limit zone. Good thing this stretch of roads wasn't heavily patrolled. He didn't need a ticket or two. Explaining those to either of his two law enforcement cousins, Sheriff Dakota Knox or Deputy Police Chief Logan Jones, wasn't something he planned on starting out his new life with.

Carlos popped Ingrid's car trunk open. Inside were two boxes from the butcher shop. Four bags from the farmer's market and six cartons from the main market in town. Where was Peter?

"There's more in the backseat." Ingrid grabbed two bags out of the passenger front seat.

"Please tell me you didn't blow budget." Carlos opened the driver's side backdoor.

"Marjorie asked me to pick up a few things for the Sadie Hawkins event. I'm helping her and Agatha with the event. MacGruder's is hosting this time. Blue Moon Sadie Hawkins."

"Did you mention this to Peter? Let him know?" Carlos grabbed four of the bags filling the remainder of the backseat.

"Might have. You and he were busy running out to the house. Off to the bank. A couple of trips to Sylvan Valley. Whirlwind visits." Ingrid set her two bags on the kitchen table. "You didn't tell me Peter bought MacGruder's until after he headed back to Los Angeles."

Carlos placed his bags on the kitchen counter. He turned and leaned against the counter. "You didn't tell him the last time you talked?"

"*The last time we talked, Carlos Gabriel Ramirez, was when Peter and I hugged goodbye his last visit.*" Ingrid closed the space between her and Carlos until they stood toe to toe. She jabbed her finger in his stomach. "You might have told him yourself."

"Ingrid, I didn't know until you just told me." Carlos clenched Ingrid's hand. "You can stop poking me."

"Maybe another poke or two will remind you." Ingrid yanked her hand free. "Siobhan Jones is redoing Sadie's. Maxon's is closed until Carla, Kirk, and Daniel are back from their honeymoon. That leaves MacGruder's."

Carlos scooted by Ingrid. "Okay, I screwed up. I'll let Peter know when he gets here."

"Let me know what?" Peter asked, entering the kitchen.

"Deities on high, you know better than sneaking up on people." Carlos turned around, both hands fisted.

Peter stepped back. "I'm not sneaking. Door's open and I got stuff from out of Ingrid's car. Supposed to be helping unload."

"Yes, he is." Ingrid stepped between Carlos and Peter. "Come on, Peter. I can use your help with the heavier stuff."

Carlos lowered his fists, shook his head and followed Ingrid and Peter out the door.

Ten minutes later and several trips back and forth from the car to the house, Peter slammed Ingrid's car trunk shut. Carlos stood adjacent to the car, holding the last of the bags from out of the backseat. Peter stacked the last two cartons on top of each other and picked them up. "Now, what is it you keep putting off telling me?"

Carlos handed Ingrid the bags he held as he reached the backdoor. "Sit down and I'll explain."

"Put the cartons next to the chest freezer. I'll unpack them in a moment." Ingrid set the bags in the kitchen sink. "There's fresh coffee and Grandma Patrice's peachy jam muffins on the table."

Peter set the cartons next to the freezer and walked to the table where Carlos sat pouring coffee into three mugs. "I hope that's decaf. I need to sleep tonight."

Carlos pushed the plate of muffins across the table to Peter. "I drink only decaf. I sleep at night. Only all-nighters are full moon and even then, I'm probably in bed before the moon sets."

Peter saluted Carlos with his mug and sipped his coffee. "Sleep is wonderful when you get eight hours REM filled with delicious dreams. Like—well, maybe I best not do full disclosure."

"Peter Griffin Drake TMI!" Ingrid called out. "TMI!"

Carlos set his mug down and burst out laughing. "Got ya, cuz."

Peter glanced at Ingrid, who held up five fingers and went back to emptying the cartons.

"*Now* I want to know what either of you ain't fessing up to." Peter pushed the plate of muffins back to the middle of the table.

Carlos leaned back in his chair, grinning. "Shortlist. MacGruder's is yours. Sale closed and settled last week. Blue moon happening next Saturday and..." Carlos paused.

Ingrid sat in the chair opposite Peter and Carlos. "Drama is useless. Tell Peter what he's walking into."

"Walking into?" Peter gawked at Carlos, then Ingrid.

"Yeah," Ingrid began, reaching for a muffin. "You're hosting the Blue Moon Halloween Sadie Hawkins event."

"Sadie Hawkins?" Peter broke a muffin in half and took a bite. He sipped his coffee and swallowed.

"Sadie Hawkins is ladies' choice full moon event." Ingrid set her mug on the table. "Early on, both Cauldron Falls and Sylvan Valley folks didn't mix much. Sylvan MacKenzie and Hendrik Cauldron's wives planned and hosted the first intertown event first full moon of the year."

"Let the women choose who they were interested in. Some of the men got to choose if there were unpaired folks by the end of the event." Carlos laid his hand on Ingrid's. "Met Ingrid that way."

"Matchmakers got involved as population grew, more folks settled in each town, and some humans joined us." Ingrid leaned over and kissed Carlos's cheek.

"Sounds like fun." Peter set his empty mug on the table.

"Magic is always present. Supernaturals and magics energies mix. Auras ignite, love magic sparks, and matches happen." Ingrid gathered the mugs and placed them in the sink. "Humans give off their own magic in their auras."

"How involved do I have to be?" Peter pushed back from the table.

"Be present, make rounds, host, and feed those that show up." Carlos put the remaining muffins in the refrigerator. "Ingrid, RSVPs are required, right?"

"Yes. Helps with food count. Crowd control and the matchmakers. They record every match." Ingrid tossed diced carrots, celery, and onion in the double-handled pot on the stove. She added salt and pepper as she continued speaking. "Most are thirty-day trials. Some are renewals."

"I'll be back in a moment. Need to get my suitcase and backpack out of the car." Peter opened the backdoor and turned back. "Trials? Renewals?

Carlos grinned. "Sure, try each other out. Date, get acquainted and if it works, renew at the next full moon."

"Carlos, that's current vernacular." Ingrid shook her head. "Matchmaking based on courting and sparking. Approval is the couple's choice and matchmaker recorded."

"I'll ask my questions when I get back." Peter closed the door behind him. What had he walked into? Happened upon? Gracious Lupa, how much didn't he know? How much did he know?

Peter set his suitcase and backpack on the hood of his car. He slowly inhaled and exhaled. Five-star world-class chefs didn't panic. Didn't lose their cool. They handled things. How for the love of Lupa and the One, did he handle this? Get a crash course on Sadie Hawkins events Cauldron Falls style? Oh blast, did Sylvan Valley do theirs differently? Crowd control? Mixed crowd from Cauldron Falls and Sylvan Valley or Cauldron Falls only? Peter let out a yip, low-volume growl, and bark. "I know wolf. More frustrations and surprises. Don't worry, friend. We'll do it. Make it happen just like we always do."

Peter picked up his suitcase, slung his backpack over one shoulder, and trotted into the house. Time for Q&A had come. He hoped quizzing Carlos and Ingrid revealed lots of answers. Not lots more questions.

Carlos took Peter's suitcase and backpack. "Ingrid needs your help with the mutton stew. It's your recipe."

Peter nodded. "One of the first I concocted on my own."

"Do you brown the mutton before cutting it into chunks or chunk it first?" Ingrid waved her meat cleaver in front of her.

Peter deftly moved to the side and clasped Ingrid's arm. "Rub seasoning on the mutton. Chunk it next. Brown in the vegetable juice bits and scrapings. Add a bit of water and either beer or wine. Cook for five minutes. Then add the diced potatoes and tomato paste."

"Basic vegetable soup stock base." Ingrid handed Peter the meat cleaver. "You chunk the meat. I already rubbed it down with garlic powder, thyme, basil, and nutmeg."

"Good. You want to add a half teaspoon of sugar after you add the tomato paste. Takes the acid out of it plus sweetens the beer or wine." Peter chopped the mutton roast in half. Quarters next and smaller chunks last. He added the meat to the pot and stirred.

Last time he'd made mutton stew was on the night he planned on proposing. The night he thought he and Marcella were going to consummate their engagement and pledge their futures together. Marcella never showed up. Sent him an apology letter and hocked the pearl earrings he'd given her for her birthday. Used the proceeds to pay for her elopement. Then had the audacity to ask him if he'd be the godfather to her baby girl born six months after her elopement. Marcella hadn't said she was pregnant by someone else when they met.

Any other relationships after that had smoked and fizzled out after the third or fourth date. Some women wanted the thrill of making it with a supernatural shapeshifter. He almost got hairy and growly to scare one woman off who kept trying to egg him into morphing because that was what all the horror movies she loved showed happened. Now, he was supposed to host a love magic event? How the hell did he get into this mess?

Peter stepped back from the stove. He tossed the meat cleaver in the sink. The thud echoed throughout the kitchen. Carlos trotted into the kitchen. "Everything alright?"

Ingrid nodded. "Yeah, Peter tossed something in the sink."

"Peter, you okay?" Carlos faced him.

Peter started to shrug. His wolf growled. Peter walked to the sink, rinsed his hands and dried them. "Yeah, doing great. It's going to take a bit for the broth and meat to cook."

Ingrid took a bag of yeast rolls out of the freezer and placed them in the refrigerator. "I'll pop them in the oven about ten minutes before we eat."

"Should warm them fine." Peter sat in a chair next to the table. "I've got a few questions."

Carlos placed three wine glasses on the table along with the bottle of wine he uncorked earlier. "Wine?"

"Half glass." Peter leaned back in the chair. "I bought MacGruder's knowing the renovations were half done. That was two months ago. Last update I had was three weeks more before inspection was due."

Ingrid sipped her wine and set the glass down. "Chaos descended."

"Chaos?" Peter sniffed his wine. Pulled Ingrid's glass to him and sniffed. They smelled the same. One sip and Ingrid was chaotic? She didn't appear drunk.

Carlos held up his glass. "A toast to chaos."

Ingrid touched her glass to Carlos's and sipped more wine. Peter glanced at Carlos who sipped and set his glass down. Peter repeated his question. "Chaos?"

Ingrid nodded vigorously. "Siobhan Jones closed Sadie's for minor renovations and updates. Same time Carla Smith closed Maxson's until she, Kirk Addison, and Daniel McFarmer get back from their honeymoon. That leaves MacGruder's."

"Two places under renovation. One temporarily closed. Chaos where to hold the Sadie Hawkins event. Need large enough place with it being a blue moon event for a crowd upwards to possibly seventy-five to a hundred people. Not including staff." Carlos shrugged as Peter stared at him.

"Seventy-five to a hundred? MacGruder's max capacity is twenty tables plus the lunch counter." Peter picked up his wine glass, held it up to the light, sighed, and took two swallows.

A tart red rose wine slid over his tastebuds and down his gullet. He set his glass down, pushed back from the table and stood. He walked over to the stove, stirred the stew, turned the burner down and paced back to the counter. Leaning against the counter, he continued his train of thought. "How many RSVPs are there?"

Carlos pulled a pad lying in the middle of the table to him. He drew a rectangle center of the sheet of paper. "MacGruder's prior shape fit the corner lot on Fifth Street. When the downtown regentrification started, the two shops next to it closed. Max MacGruder was in process of buying them."

Carlos drew another rectangle next to the first. Instead of horizontal, he drew it vertically. "You own both buildings. MacGruder's is twice its original size. You're renovations took longer due to connecting the two buildings and enlarging the dining area, plus adding the bar where the lunch counter was."

Peter quaffed a third of his wine and set the glass down. "Why didn't you tell me this?"

"Foremen's email with the schematics went to my spam folder. I went down and personally looked over everything with the inspector. That's why I've been trying to reach you for the last week and a half." Carlos tossed the pen on the table. "You've got room enough for two hundred people if you move tables and chairs. Parking lot has ample capacity."

Peter combed his hands through his hair. "I'm hosting a Blue Moon Sadie Hawkins event as my grand opening."

Ingrid arranged the yeast rolls on a baking sheet, placed them in the oven and set the timer. She handed Peter soup bowls and soup spoons. "Set the table, please. You aren't hosting alone."

Peter put the bowls and spoons on the table. He grabbed Ingrid's arm as she started past him. "I'm not hosting alone?"

Ingrid pulled her arm away, turned the oven timer off, and pulled the baking sheet out of the oven. "You've got help. Marjorie Smith, Agatha Clemons, and I are your co-hosts. Notices are out in the paper, posted on Cauldron Falls social media and website."

Peter dished up the stew. Mutton stew. Full moon event. Blue full moon. Legends touted full moon magic amplified during blue full moons. Had his wolf been communicating with Lupa and the One about his mate longings again? Peter muttered a quick prayer as he sat down to eat. Were his personal deities paying attention? Were they smacking him and his wolf with blatant signals—another mate was in the offing?

CHAPTER TWO

A Witch's Hesitation

Tuesday Mid-Morning

Agatha Clemons shoved the advertisement underneath the desk blotter. Two Sadie Hawkins events in one month. She had a big problem. She wasn't matched as the second paragraph of her license said she needed to be. That tall tale had turned into a yarn that fell way short of fulfillment when her make-believe match returned to town married and his spouse six months pregnant. Dang Rob Nicely for doing that. Blast him for not noticing her interest and staying in Cauldron Falls instead of going to university in Europe.

The Sister Three were supposed to host the last quarter of the year matchmaking events. Chaos erupted instead. The Sister Three Matchmakers were not hosting more events until Spring. Maggie Nickerson, Cauldron Falls top elite matchmaker, had got matched, married, and was due any day with her second child. Maggie's husband, Caleb Morningstar, headed up the MatchMakers Council's truth in advertising committee in addition to his duties as elder leader of the male matchmakers and the council's community liaison. Maggie wasn't available to host matchmaking events. Matchmakers Council decree said two or more matchmakers must be present at all Sadie Hawkins Full Moon events.

Agatha drummed her fingers on the desk. *Rat-tat-tat* echoed throughout the quiet shop. Marjorie, her best friend and business partner, was visiting a client and his match with both families present. Getting consent from the older founding families sometimes took discussions and quite a few meetings. With Marjorie out of the shop, Agatha could pace and think while she unpacked their latest shipments of teas, crystals, potion ingredients, and new tarot card decks with instruction books. Pace, plan, unpack, and check off inventory. Wear another uneven rut in the wooden floor as Marjorie referred to her think-pacing.

Agatha tossed a pad and pen on her desk. Brainstorming might turn up some ideas. She could walk, think out loud, and jot notes without Marjorie frowning at her or insisting she go do her think-pacing-talking out in the alley where clients couldn't see or hear her.

"Who's available who might fake a relationship with me?" Agatha started pacing. "Geoff? No, he moved to Sylvan Valley. He's seeing Susanna. Who else?"

Agatha paced to the wall and turned. She held up one hand, putting fingers down as each name she said crossed off the list she mentally and verbally compiled. "Frank Cormier left town. Rumor is he's back. Can't use him. Might show up. Corban Heckenger? Not my type."

Agatha set the small box of crystals on the counter she'd unboxed. "Agatha, time to describe your dream date."

She walked back to her desk, pulled the pad to her, picked up the pen and wrote as she spoke. "Close to my age. Nothing wrong with being thirty-five and available. My height or taller. Five-eight isn't bad."

She scribbled notes as she continued. "Supernatural or magic preferred. Some humans don't understand matchmaker's magic. Last couple humans I dated ran the moment they could see sparks ignite."

"Would be nice if they were lithe." Agatha smirked at her next thought. "I'm not being prudish. I walk three miles twice a week. Bike ride with my nieces and nephews a mile or two a couple times a month. Not looking for someone who's into exotic lovemaking positions."

She wrote down two more items. Could be clean-shaven or bearded. Preferred well-groomed without hair longer than shoulder length. Major preference: no buzz cuts.

Agatha laid the pen down. Okay, her dream male was five-eight, hair color unknown, eye color to be determined, and muscular build without being overly athletic. She wasn't into watching sports or participating in them beyond her nieces and nephews softball games and the occasional basketball game. "Alright, what do I name you? Something someone in Cauldron Falls isn't familiar with. Doesn't have a relative popping out of the woodwork or lives in Sylvan Valley."

She drummed the pen on the desk. Wrote four names on the pad. Whispered each aloud. Crossed two of them out. Two names were left. Agatha raised both hands heavenward as she spoke her prayer and invocation aloud. "Luna and the One, I will look for a match at the event. Please help me choose a name that leads me forward. Help me get through the event. I need your help."

She glanced at the two names. She closed her eyes, trailed her finger up and down the pad three times and stopped. Her finger landed between the two names. She had a first and last name. Peter Griffin. The story would be if asked, she'd recently broken off a long-distance relationship and was looking for a new match. She wouldn't say who she'd broke off with. She had a name if pressed.

The door of Moonlit Matches and Magic swung open. Marjorie stormed inside, cussing and fussing. "Blasted stuck in a rut parents. Grown children who can't stand on their own two feet and make a decision." Marjorie tossed the folder she carried and her tote on her desk, pulled out her desk chair and dropped into it. She reached down, pulled off her shoes and swung her feet up on her desk.

Agatha walked over to the shop's front door and turned the open sign over to 'Out for Lunch'. She opened the mini fridge behind her desk, pulled out a diet soda, opened it and set it in front of Marjorie. "Need a cup?"

Marjorie shook her head. "Not at the moment. If it weren't business hours, I'd tell you come on we're finding somewhere to drown my frustrations with something stronger."

"Better to eat lunch, consume a few carbs, and a bit of chocolate. Keeps you ready for the next client who walks in." Agatha laid three chocolate kisses on the desk. "What do you want for lunch? My turn to pay."

Marjorie swung her feet off the desk. "There's a new place opening up across the street from MacGruder's."

"Two eateries next door to each other? Bad for business." Agatha picked up her cell phone off her desk.

"Mitchell's is a bakery. Pre-made sandwiches for breakfast and lunch. MacGruder's is lunch and dinner." Marjorie pulled a flyer out of her tote bag and pushed it across the desk to Agatha. "Fran Mitchell is making the cakes and sweets for our Sadie Hawkins event."

Agatha pulled the flyer to her. Sheet cakes, layer cakes, custom cakes, donuts, and other assorted sweets and breads with their prices ran down one side. The other was the sandwich price list. Bottom third listed condiments and drinks. "Quite an assortment. What do we try?"

"Turkey, cranberry sauce, arugula and swiss on pumpernickel. Pumpkin pie cheesecake bar." Marjorie sipped her soda.

Agatha circled the items on the flyer, dialed the number and placed their order. "Will be here in about twenty minutes. Wanna fill me in on your meeting?"

"Thought my clients were ready to sign their pre-nup agreement. Assuming got me in a world of confusion. Both sets of parents didn't like certain parts. Grandparents cussed and demanded answers to why a prenup was needed." Marjorie sighed. "Kicker was wanting to see my license and know who *my* match was. I'm glad Terrence is out of town. Or they would be demanding his presence."

Agatha squirmed. Demands to see matchmaker licenses had increased with the Matchmakers Council decree going public. Proof of matches seemed to be on the rise regardless of how long the matchmaker been in business and their reputation. Some swore Maggie Nickerson caused the decree. Many muttered Maggie's marrying Caleb

Morningstar should have squelched the issue. Maggie's trainees and assistants went on to get their licenses and record their matches. Nothing said matchmaker's personal matches had to last for a specific period. If her secret got out, a double chaotic whirlwind would explode. Keeping secrets from your best friend was one thing. Keeping them from your business partner was another. Especially when it affected your business reputation and vitality.

"Did the mail come?" Marjorie stood, moving toward where Agatha usually stacked the mail.

"Advertisements. A couple of bills. I put them in the file with the bank statement and checkbook. Figured we could go over them after lunch." Agatha glanced at her watch. "Lunch is due shortly."

Marjorie sat in one of the chairs in front of Agatha's desk. "Did you see the flyer that Lincoln came up with for the event? He got the post office to deliver one to every address in town. Should be in today's mail."

Agatha stood between Marjorie and the desk. Agatha pulled the flyer out from under the blotter and held it out. "Is this it?"

Marjorie grabbed the flyer. "Sure is. Why were you hiding it?"

"Not really hiding it. Putting it out of sight." Agatha leaned against the desk, folding her arms tightly across her chest.

"I don't get it." Marjorie laid the flyer on the desk. "Blue moons don't happen often. Two full moons in the same month plus Halloween is awesome for us."

"Yeah, I know. Double business exposure. More clients." Agatha sat in her desk chair. "Word of mouth advertising. All great marketing with little or no expense."

Agatha covered her face with her hands. She slowly inhaled and exhaled. Did she fess up? Keep on faking things? Or both?

Agatha lowered her hands. "Marjorie, there's something you need to know."

"Oh?"

"Yeah." Agatha stood, walked around the desk and started pacing. "I'm not sure where to begin."

"At the beginning," Marjorie said, as the shop door opened.

"Delivery for Agatha Clemons." The teenage male set the plastic bag on the counter. "My mom, Fran Mitchell, sent along a couple of cake samples for you. You can tell her which one you want for the centerpiece cake."

Marjorie rose. "You must be Reynold. Fran's middle boy."

The teen smiled and nodded. "Yeah. If you're gonna tip, can you do it in cash?"

Marjorie snorted. "Easier to spend."

"No, easier to put in the bank on my way back after my other deliveries. Otherwise, gotta wait till Mom writes my paycheck. Gotta keep a few bucks handy when you're taking your gal out."

Agatha smirked. She pulled a five and a couple of singles out of her wallet. "Here's extra. You take my niece, Alisha, someplace nice."

Reynold ducked his head. "Will do, ma'am."

"Here's another five." Marjorie handed Reynold the five. "Check back in a couple days, Reynold. Mr. Franklin from the cinema owes me a couple of discount movie coupon booklets."

"Thank you, Ms. Smith. Alisha and I both thank you. What do I owe you for the tickets?"

"Nothing as long as you tell them where you got them. Moonlit Matches."

"We could come up with a couple of t-shirts for them to wear." Agatha started toward the hallway leading to the store room.

"Will tell where got tickets if asked. No shirts. Alisha and I aren't match-ready." Reynold practically ran out the door.

Marjorie opened the bag and set their lunches on the desk. She sat in the chair close to her and pointed at Agatha. "You've got two choices. Spill your *pacing* story or eat and tell me what's going on without spoiling my lunch. What's it going to be?'

Agatha locked the shop door, walked back to her desk, and slowly sank into her desk chair. Marjorie's emphasis on pacing meant one thing. She wanted the pacing story Reynold interrupted. Not her pacing dream boyfriend-building story.

Agatha slowly unwrapped her sandwich. She took a bite, chewed and swallowed. Agatha retrieved a soda from the mini fridge, opened it, and drank. She set the soda on the desk and sighed. "They say spilling your gut is good for you. Don't know that's true when it ignites a large column of chaos."

"How about you trickle things out? You know, slow and easy." Marjorie pointed at her sandwich. "Lunchtime. Eat and talk. Not smoke us out of here. Okay?"

Agatha nodded and resumed eating. She finished half her sandwich before she spoke again several minutes later. "How many times have you had to show your matchmaking license? Tell who your match is?"

Marjorie laid her sandwich down and wiped her mouth. "A lot more since Maggie's incident last Solstice. You?"

"I haven't had many appointments or clients. Busy here at the shop." Agatha shrugged and continued speaking. "Most of our clients ask for you. You got a lot of public exposure taking on a few of Maggie's assistants and getting them fully trained."

"Your license is current, right?" Marjorie finished her sandwich.

"Sorta." Agatha hastily took two bites of the remaining half of her sandwich.

"*Sorta?*" Marjorie set her soda down. "Did you let it lapse again?"

Agatha shook her head, chewed and swallowed. She tried to take another bite when Marjorie leaned forward. "Stop stalling. Is or isn't your license current?"

Agatha swallowed, grabbed her soda and drank. She burped as she started to speak. "Sorry. My license is current. Always has been. The not current part is..."

"Agatha, stop stalling." Marjorie stood. "Whatever it is, we can work it out."

Agatha glanced at Marjorie and looked away. "No current match."

"No current match?"

"Yeah."

"Recent breakup?"

"No."

"Ten months ago? By-laws allow a cooling-off period. Usually ten months."

"Longer than that."

"*Longer?*"

"Yes." Agatha gathered the trash and tossed it in the wastebasket next to the mini fridge. "About eighteen months."

"*What?*" Marjorie clapped her hand over her mouth and sat down. "What about the dude who was over in Europe?"

"Rob Nicely?" Agatha started pacing. "He had the audacity to come back with a six-month pregnant wife."

Marjorie sipped her soda and sat back down. "Agatha Clemons, you've got some explaining to do."

Agatha paced to the front door and back to her desk. "Mark Goldberg moved. Doug Huntley wasn't interested in committing. Others, there was no spark. No aura blast. Nothing beyond admiring the eye candy."

Marjorie sighed. "You know we're going to be asked at the event."

"Yeah, that's where this comes in." Agatha dropped the pad with her dream boyfriend on it on the desk in front of Marjorie.

Marjorie pulled the pad to her. She read the pad, glanced at Agatha, and shoved it back across the desk. "Another made-up boyfriend? Agatha, that didn't work last time."

"This time is different."

Marjorie shook her head, leaned back in the chair, and let go a long, slow groan. "Why do I have a feeling this is going to be complex?"

"No. Simple, easy, and quick." Agatha sat down.

"I'm listening." Marjorie downed the last of her soda and broke off a piece of her pumpkin cheesecake bar. "I'm waiting to eat this until I've heard all you have to say."

Agatha nodded. She held up three fingers. "Peter Griffin broke off with me recently. Long distance relationship." Agatha lowered two fingers. "I find a match at the event."

Marjorie tossed the piece of cheesecake bar in her mouth, chewed, and swallowed. She held up four fingers. "One, evidence of the match. Two, how you going to do that? Three, if the council finds out."

"What's four?"

Marjorie lowered her finger. "I'm nuts thinking this might work out. There's a slight jar to the plan."

"How so?"

"Agatha, MacGruder's new owner is named Peter G. Drake. People are going to think the two of you split up."

"Chaos twisted twice!"

"Have you seen or met Peter Drake?"

"No. I could change my dream boyfriend's name."

"How about you don't want to talk about the break up? Not say his name." Marjorie handed one-half of the cheesecake bar to Agatha. "Another problem is what if the RSVPs are enough for those looking for matches. Overflow isn't going to be available for you to try and woo someone."

"How many times are there overflow? Plus or minus in the number of RSVPs?" Agatha bit into the cheesecake bar, grinning as she chewed.

"We're gonna have to fudge numbers on the match sheets. Make sure there's extra RSVPs. I'll check with my cousin Lenny." Marjorie held up her hand as Agatha vehemently shook her head. "Lenny will make sure his brother George comes. You and George get along."

"Get along as well as oil and water. If I have to fake interest, George and I share a few common interests." Agatha finished her half of the cheesecake bar and wiped her mouth and hands on her napkin. "Maybe Luna and the One heard my invocation and prayer."

"Did you say your invocation and prayer before or after you decided on your fake boyfriend's name?" Marjorie tossed her napkin and empty soda can in the trash.

"Uhm—afterwards." Agatha grimaced. "No, I didn't do what you think I did."

Marjorie nodded, picking up her tote and folder. "Yes, I do. You asked. Your psyche and heart were asking before you even muttered a name. You got your answer, Agatha."

"I don't know this Peter Griffin. I made him up." Agatha started pacing again.

"You know of him. You heard his first name. Luna and the One might be giving you more information with this Griffin name. You got your nudge. You got your answer."

"Blessed Luna, what do I do now?" Agatha reached for the pad.

Marjorie grabbed it. "No going back now. You best hope Peter G. Drake is good-looking, open to a match and is ready to grab you up."

"Give me the pad." Agatha lunged for the pad.

Marjorie held it above her head. "Nothing doing. You know, once you say an invocation and prayer, you can't undo it. You can ask for another try once the answer is revealed. Right now, you won't know until you meet Peter G. Drake in the flesh. Maybe even kiss each other several times."

Agatha pulled her planner out of the middle desk drawer and slapped it on the desk. She leafed open to the day. "Two P.M. Meeting with Ingrid Ramirez. It's almost two. We've got cake to taste. Finalize decorations, food, and timeline for cutting off RSVPs. We don't say *nothing* about my match situation. *Got it? Get it? Good!*"

"You don't need to yell. Ingrid doesn't need to know. She's helping Fran Mitchell with the catering part. Fran's oldest son, Randall, is

MacGruder's bartender. Your secret is safe with me." Marjorie slipped her shoes on.

Agatha pulled her notebook out of her tote. "I'm sorry I didn't tell you before. I didn't think the matchmaker having a match would go viral. Blasted social media and Cauldron Falls predilection for non-magical items."

Marjorie laughed as she unlocked the shop's door. "Well, that predilection is a driving part of our marketing. Fuels word of mouth, people sharing their experiences. With the trinkets shop—teas, potions, and the occasional tarot reading plus crystals, help with keeping our costs and overhead down."

"Yeah, I know. I unpacked the latest shipment. We're going to need a tarot card reader. A witchy one. Mortals can do it some. Folks are going to expect full-blown magic at the event." Agatha shoved the planner in the middle drawer and pushed it closed. She brushed the crumbs and paper bits left from their lunch into the delivery bag and tossed it in the trash.

"Maybe Ingrid or Fran can do it. I hope one of them is a member of the Matchmakers Guild. Professional licenses all around are going to be inspected by attendees. Probably by Peter G. Drake and his staff, too." Marjorie grinned as she laid out the menu plans along with napkins and plastic forks next to the four cake samples Fran Mitchell sent.

"Guess I'm going to have to practice my tarot reading skills." Agatha shoved a plastic sleeve protector across the desk. Inside it was a recent tarot reader card license and a certificate passing basic tarot reading.

Marjorie burst out laughing. "You can't do both at the same time. That is only for the non-full moon match events. This isn't it."

"Let's hire one from the Guild. We can afford it. Please, let's take the easy way on this." Agatha stuffed the plastic sleeve protector back in her tote.

"I'll do it if..." Marjorie stopped speaking.

"If what?" Agatha looked away, hoping she wasn't walking into another chaotic twist.

Marjorie leaned close, whispering as Fran Mitchell and Ingrid Ramirez entered the shop. "If you openly declare in front of everyone attending, you want Peter G. Drake as your match."

Agatha placed both hands on the desk, smiling as she replied. "You think it's that easy?"

CHAPTER THREE

Event Preparations

Tuesday Afternoon

"Hello, Fran and Ingrid. You're right on time." Agatha moved past Marjorie. Agatha shoved one hand into her jeans pocket. She fisted and unfisted her hand. She held out her other, ready to shake hands with Fran and Ingrid. Blast Marjorie for tossing down the gauntlet. Marjorie's cheesy Cheshire cat grin meant she would goad and keep reminding until Agatha took action. Agatha exhaled slowly as she closed the space between her, Fran, and Ingrid.

Fran clasped her hand and let go. "I cleared my calendar. Wouldn't miss this. Mitchell's first Sadie Hawkins event. Gonna put the bakery out there. Great advertising and marketing plan. Bound to get a few commitments before the evening's over. Got business cards ordered. Flyers ready."

Ingrid touched Agatha's arm. "Brought the checklist with me we agreed to from our last meeting. Fran and I met earlier today to go over the catering list. Randall is talking with Peter about liquor and miscellaneous beverages besides coffee, tea, and water."

Marjorie moved up beside Agatha, whispering. "Hmmm, Peter G. Drake is even more into this than you knew. Luna and the One definitely heard your invocation and prayer. Your answer is here big time."

Agatha reached over, slipped her hand behind Marjorie and pinched her arm. Marjorie flinched, quickly moving away from Agatha. "Fran, good to see you. Ingrid glad you made it. I'm going to make some tea. I'll be right back. Agatha, can you help me please?"

Marjorie paused at the entrance to the hall leading to the back room. Agatha shook her head and walked past. Agatha plugged the coffee maker in, put a fresh filter in and filled it with loose tea. She turned, holding out the empty carafe to Marjorie. "Go fill this, please. *Don't* say anything more about Peter G. Drake. That is three dirty words for the next six hours. *Don't* even text me about him, my invocation and prayer, or what my secret is."

Marjorie took the carafe and walked to the sink of the back room small kitchen unit. "*Don't* think this is over. *I'm not the one with the secret that could make or break this event and our business!*"

Marjorie filled the carafe, handed it back to Agatha, and swiftly exited the back room.

Agatha emptied the carafe into the coffee maker, clicked it on and leaned against the small work table the coffee maker sat on. Her grandmother's and mother's constant refrain of honesty makes the best policy echoed through her mind as Agatha counted with each breath she took.

Transparency worked to a point. She got people wanted success, wanted a guarantee—except matchmakers didn't promise guarantees. No money changed hands until the wedding or contractual negotiations were underway. Why did people expect, demand, or want to know about their matchmaker's personal life? Number of successful matches, yes. Successful prenup agreements and wedding planning, yes. Those were the core elements of their business. Love magic happened on its own between the two or more people attracted to each other. The one some asked Luna and the One to guide them to. Nothing was a hundred percent. Life came with ups and downs. Ebbs and flows. Deities presented gifts daily. It was up to the receivers to use the gift.

"Agatha, the tea almost ready?" Marjorie called out.

Agatha flexed her hands, straightened, and checked the coffee maker. The brew cycle was almost done. "A couple more minutes. I'm getting the mugs, sugar, and stirrers."

Only patience and calm would get her and Marjorie through this meeting. Luna, she hoped Marjorie hadn't said anything to Fran and Ingrid.

Marjorie pulled two more chairs up to Agatha's desk. "I hope you brought the price list for the food. We've only got a few days to get the order in."

Ingrid pulled two sheets of paper out of her portfolio. "Peter and Carlos were discussing that when I left. Peter knows the event is his grand opening. He's insistent on doing the meal prep and hiring extra help as needed. Carlos told him that he needed to relax. Let us first get the final lists and items needed figured out."

Marjorie smiled, taking the sheets Ingrid handed her. So Peter was a hands-on owner. That meant he'd probably be there front and center Halloween night. Marjorie glanced over her shoulder. Luna and the One were answering Agatha's invocation and prayer in a huge way.

Marjorie laid the sheets on the desk and sat in the chair next to Ingrid. "Steak tartare. Several pork and beef roasts. Red potatoes au gratin. Tossed salad. Corn and pea medley. Vegetarian Lasagna. Vegan dish: Spaghetti squash with marinara sauce and roasted pine nuts."

"A bit for everyone. Carlos suggested a soup of some sort. Fall harvest is happening. I asked one of my neighbors about using their unsaleable butternut squash. I can get enough squash to make a soup entree that vegetarians or vegans can eat. Even the meat eaters." Ingrid opened her portfolio and scribbled notes on the pad inside.

"Marjorie," Agatha called out. "Can you help me please?"

"One moment, Fran and Ingrid. I'll be right back." Marjorie rose and entered the back room.

Agatha pointed to the tray holding four mugs filled with tea, box of sugar cubes, and stirrers. "Did you get the paper plates I reminded you about? For the cake and sweets tasting?"

"In the cabinet where we keep them for lunch usage." Marjorie picked up the tray. "Think you can handle the plates and napkins?"

"Oh, yes. They're so heavy. I will do my best to not drop them." Agatha stuck her tongue out and blew a raspberry. "*Pfffffft.*"

Marjorie shook her head and exited carrying the tray.

Agatha high-fived herself. Letting go felt good. She followed Marjorie into the front of the shop.

Marjorie passed the food menu to Agatha as she sat down. "Anything on there we need to add to or take off?"

"Are we going to have the ingredient cards for each item posted? Allergies and food preferences?" Agatha pointed to the tossed salad items. "Is this with dressing or without?"

"Without. Peter mentioned that when I showed him the menu." Ingrid flipped a page over on her notepad. She ran her finger down the page, stopped part way, and looked up. "Balsamic or Thousand Island is what he suggested. A bit of tartness with a raspberry or orange mix for the Balsamic. Bottled Thousand Island. Not enough time to make his own and let it set."

Agatha added two sugar cubes to her tea, stirred and sipped. "How many roasts did we decide upon?"

"Fifteen thin sliced. Enough for everyone to get a few slices of each and seconds if they want. Timing is important to all of this, too. People are going to need time to mingle, scope each other out and eat." Fran laid two charts on the desk. "Initial half-hour mingle. Find a possible dining partner. Dinner hour and a half. First dance twenty minutes. Dessert course half hour. Second dance twenty minutes. More mingling and match recording for those making a thirty-day match. Possibly one more dance, men's choice, if there are still unpartnered folks left."

"I think we can eliminate the Steak tartare. Cooked food keeps better. Salad can be made morning of. Last Sadie Hawkins event ran until close to two a.m. What time are we starting?" Agatha laid her planner on the desk. "Full moon rise is around eightish. Peaks close to midnight. Are we going to have the skylight available for people declaring their match in the moonlight?'

Ingrid smirked. "No skylight. Roof had to be redone. Patio off the party room has a pergola that will let the moonlight through. That is as close to declaring match in moonlight as possible."

Agatha made notes in her planner as she spoke. "Weather is going to play key role that night. We're going to need a moon effect spotlight over where we intend to record the matches. Are we going to have a justice of the peace present? A high priestess? Full moon marriage ceremonies?"

"Probably no justice of the peace or high priestess or marriage ceremonies. Matchmaking event only." Ingrid looked up from her notes. "Peter isn't familiar with Cauldron Falls full moon events. He's asked a lot of questions. Some probably from curiosity. Most from a business aspect."

Marjorie rapped on the desk. Fran, Ingrid and Agatha looked at her. "Peter is going to be the major decision-maker on some things. No way around it. His place. His space and his business reputation first impression happening."

Agatha nodded. "Ingrid do you know what MacGruder's capacity is with the renovations?"

"Carlos said the inspector estimated one hundred to a hundred and fifty standing room. We're going to have tables and chairs, serving area, and dance floor. Probably need to limit RSVPs to eighty?" Ingrid laid a schematic sketch of MacGruder's floor plan middle of the papers. "Maybe seventy."

Fran turned the floor plan toward her. "How about this? We use the bar area for food and drinks. Have the buffet set up adjacent to the bar? Randall and his assistant manning the bar. Two to three servers for the buffet line. Another three to four for clearing."

Marjorie pointed to the open area near the patio doors. "Randall could mark names off as they come in, give them their drink and meal tickets. Agatha and I can set up middle of the back wall close to the dance area. I think we could accommodate sixty-five to seventy people. Going to be a few no-shows. Cost to person is meal, drink, and entrance fee. About a hundred and twenty-five dollars per person is what Agatha and I figured."

"Here's the initial cost Peter came up with." Ingrid showed the accounting sheet to Agatha and Marjorie. "He's picking up half of the cost since it's his grand opening. The remainder is overhead costs. Half of that is your deposit. Anything over the balance owing is profit. Peter may be willing to offset a bit more since I am helping out with the catering and preparation."

Fran laid her expense sheet on the table. "Your deposit will cover the centerpiece cake, brownies, and assorted cookies. I'm donating two sheet layer cakes and a large pan of brandied bread pudding."

Agatha stood and paced from her desk to the front door and back. "Quick rounding of cost numbers and possible RSVPs numbers needed, break even might be possible. Can we agree this is going to be business expense and small profit margins?"

Fran nodded. "Yes. I'm on board."

"I'm on board, too." Ingrid glanced at her watch. "Shortest business meeting I've been to in quite a while."

Marjorie chortled. "Ladies, I'm in as well. Agatha, your vote?"

"In and figuring we need to make sure that the price is on the website right away. The flyer went out in today's mail." Agatha picked up her phone. "I'll call Lincoln to get the ticket portal ready and list the price."

Agatha stepped into the back room as she dialed Lincoln's number.

"Graphics and Marketing. Lincoln speaking."

"Hi, Lincoln. It's Agatha." Agatha glanced at the calendar laying on the work table. "How soon can you update the ticket portal and our website?"

"This afternoon if you've got the information ready. You can email it to me."

"Let me give you the specifics now. I'll follow up with an email in a bit. Ticket price per person is one hundred twenty-five dollars. Price includes buffet dinner and dessert plus coffee and tea. Cash bar available. ID will be checked. Pay at time of purchase to secure RSVP spot. Limited RSVP spots available. Event not open to public."

"Sounds like you are limiting folks. Let me confirm this. Price a hundred twenty-five per head. Price includes dinner and dessert buffet with tea and coffee. Cash bar. ID checked. Buy now. Pay now to secure your RSVP. Limited RSVP available. Closed event." Lincoln rattled off time frame to update website and ticket portal. "Client walked in. I'll text when I've got everything updated. Bye."

Agatha laid her phone on the desk. "Lincoln has the basics. He's updating the Moonlit Matches website and ticket portal this afternoon. I'll send him an email with any changes we need and verbiage updates. Everything will go live tomorrow morning, okay?"

Fran and Ingrid nodded.

Marjorie sorted the papers into three stacks. "First stack is accounting items. Second stack is menu items. Third is layout."

Ingrid's phone danced and vibrated across the desk. It stopped, chimed twice and vibrated again. Ingrid picked up her phone, smiled and laid the phone down. "Peter and Carlos are at MacGruder's. Peter's invited us to check out the party room and patio."

"We can do that after we taste the cake. Finalize the menu, and ad verbiage. Fran, does Lincoln do your website?" Agatha opened the first cake sample box. She cut the sample into four pieces.

"He does. Our hosting service handles updates. I'll have the hosting service reach out to him for URL links and updates. Agatha, thanks for overseeing that." Fran took a sheet out of her portfolio. She laid it on the desk. "What's the number on this box?"

Marjorie held up the box. "Number three."

"Number three is a buttercream frosting. Vanilla cake with cherries and chocolate bits. The frosting in between layers contains either chocolate or cherries."

Marjorie tasted her piece. " Frosting is smooth sweetness with a hint of vanilla. Cherries and chocolate mix together, adding a second burst of sweetness that doesn't overwhelm the cake."

"I agree." Agatha laid her fork down. "Not sure we want it that light with possibly strong tasters. Some will come back for more, wanting that sugar rush to get through the evening."

Ingrid made a note on the paper Fran hand the other samples listed on. "Let's try sample four. It's amaretto with expresso cream cheese frosting. Chocolate and white layers."

Marjorie cut the sample into four pieces. Each tasted their piece.

Fran nodded. "This is a stronger taste. Sugar ripples across your taste buds as the expresso and amaretto mix. I think this one with a chocolate mix for the layers might be a better option."

Agatha sipped her tea. "Three is out. Four is the leader."

Ingrid pointed to the sample marked number one. "Orange cream cheese frosting. Orange frosting between layers and orange-yellow cake mix."

Each tried the sample. Ingrid nodded. "Tart and sweet. This might do well as a sheet cake. Gives a bit of kick without overwhelming."

Marjorie and Agatha agreed. Fran pulled sample two to the center of the desk. "This is a plum raspberry cake. Plum middle with raspberry frosting. It's mild in taste and has a sugar rush as you eat it."

Agatha shook her head as she tasted the sample. "Not a combination that rolls across my tastebuds. Probably an acquired taste."

"I agree with Agatha." Marjorie wiped her mouth. "Ingrid, what do you think?"

"I'm going to answer as a shapeshifter. Too tart and too sweet are not going to go over. I think sheet cakes should be three and one.

Four the centerpiece cake." Ingrid tapped the sheet. "How about butterscotch blondies for the brownies? Cookies might be shortbread, chocolate chip, and oatmeal raisin."

Fran held up her pen. "I've got it. How about a pumpkin pie cheesecake sheet cake? Second sheet cake sample number one. I like Ingrid's butterscotch blondies and cookies suggestions."

"All in favor, raise your hand." Agatha wrote Fran's sweets and cake list on the blank top of the sheet from her side. Fran, Ingrid and Marjorie raised their hands. Agatha raised hers.

"Looks like we got the sweets and cake list handled." Fran put the list in her portfolio.

Ingrid finished her tea. "Are we good on the menu now? No steak tartare. The rest of it, okay?"

"I think we need both dressings to give choices. Not more than the two Peter suggested." Marjorie pulled the menu sheet out from the menu pile. "Any other changes or additions?"

"I'm good." Agatha put the mugs on the tray along with the paper plates and forks.

"Me too," added Fran.

"Okay, that leaves us with the verbiage and website updates." Agatha took the checklist sheet out of her folder. "Lincoln is adding the basics like I said. What we need to decide is how we want the invite to appear on each of our websites. Ingrid, has Peter updated MacGruder's website?"

Ingrid sighed. "He hasn't. Carlos and I did. Peter hasn't seen it yet. There may be a few tweaks."

Marjorie leaned back in her chair. "We're working with a short timeline. Today is Tuesday. Saturday is Halloween."

Agatha jotted notes as Marjorie continued speaking. "Ticket portal goes live today. Our websites updated today. We cut tickets off at midnight Friday."

"Here's a quick take on verbiage." Agatha picked up her sheet and read. "MacGruder's Grand Opening Saturday Night Full Moon Event. Halloween at its best. Private Sadie Hawkins Blue Moon Dinner Dance. Moonlit Matches Matchmakers. Dinner and Dessert Buffet. Tea, coffee and soft drinks included. Grab your tickets now. Portal is open. Limited RSVPs available."

"I like it." Fran nodded. "Could we fit in each of our business names?"

"I'm either part of Mitchell's or MacGruder's. I help out where I can when I'm needed," Ingrid stated.

Agatha hastily crossed through things. Wrote a few more lines and read the redone verbiage. "Don't miss out on MacGruder's Private Blue Moon Event Saturday Night. Halloween at its best. Sadie Hawkins Dinner Dance sponsored by Moonlit Matches, Mitchell's Bakery and MacGruder's. Matchmakers on hand. Dinner and Dessert Buffet. Tea, coffee and soft drinks included. Grab your tickets now. Portal is open. Limited RSVPs available."

"What about ticket cost?" Marjorie asked.

"On the ticket page along with event time when they click to purchase." Agatha laid the sheet on the paper. "Easy and quick. Tell em what's happening. Where and when."

"Sounds like we're agreed on price, number of RSVPs, and ad verbiage. What about event time?" Ingrid started gathering up her papers.

"Six to one? Doors open at five-thirty." Marjorie drew a circle on the paper in front of her. Divided the circle in half and the halves in half. "Setup and tear down, a couple hours."

"Things will overlap some. Peter will have staff doing clean up and helping with the setup. Siobhan Jones dropped off the decorations from the last Sadie Hawkins. I've got a few pumpkins, tea lights and other fall items we can use." Fran made a quick note on the sheet of paper clipped to the front of her portfolio.

"We can tweak things after we look over the party room and patio. We might want to forgo outdoor full-moon declarations. Do them inside with a full moon spotlight near the matchmaker's station." Ingrid glanced at her watch. "Carlos said we could come over around three. Let's continue our discussion there once we've seen the layout."

Marjorie rose. "Good idea, Ingrid. Let's go."

Agatha hung back as the others made their way toward the door. "I'll be along in a moment. Need to get my sweater."

"I'll get mine, too." Marjorie started back across the shop. "We'll meet you in front of MacGruder's in five minutes."

"See you there." Ingrid and Fran waved and exited the shop.

Agatha pulled her fanny pack out of her bottom desk drawer, shoved the drawer closed and rushed into the back room. She fastened her fanny pack around her waist, grabbed her sweater off the coat hooks near the back door, and flung the door open.

Blaring beeps erupted. Bright strobe lights flashed on and off. Jolting echoing beeps continued. Agatha fumbled along the wall. Where was the damn fire alarm keypad?

Bright flashes illuminated the keypad further down the wall. Agatha pressed her hands flat against the wall, making her way toward the square red keypad. She reached out, ready to key in the code.

Silence blasted sounds away. Agatha shook her head, blinked and turned. She squinted as her vision cleared. Marjorie stood close to the kitchen unit close to the back room entrance. She pointed at the blue square keypad on the wall next to her. "Setting off the burglar alarm isn't going to keep you from meeting Peter G. Drake. You can explain why you set off the burglar alarm once the police get here. I hope Sheriff Knox and Deputy Police Chief Jones buy your story."

CHAPTER FOUR

Shapeshifter's Secrets

Tuesday Late Afternoon

"Thanks, Dakota." Peter turned, facing his other cousin, Logan. "Thank you too, Logan. I appreciate you stopping by. And for not issuing Ingrid's business partner a violation."

"The alarm got turned off before central dispatch sent out the alert." Sheriff Dakota Knox chuckled. "Good thing Logan and I stopped by. Other than a noise complaint, nothing illegal going on."

Deputy Police Chief Logan Jones held out his hand. "Peter, MacGruder's is looking good. Your fire and theft alarms work fine. The silent robbery alarm test passed muster. Cauldron Falls central dispatch and Sylvan Valley central dispatch report receiving all three alarm reports."

Peter clasped Logan's hand and tugged. Logan smiled as he moved into Peter's hug.

"Cousin, I wish I'd taken you up on the offer to visit more often. Los Angeles is okay. Most of the time, it's fine. Sunshine and warmth." Peter released his embrace and stepped back.

Dakota tapped Peter's shoulder. "Hugs are good, cousin. The few times I visited San Francisco, it was okay. Missed the smell of the earth. The fall scents of foliage as it decomposes. Color changes."

Peter hugged Dakota. "Most days Los Angeles smells of smoke, car fumes and air so damn filthy, a good stiff breeze coughs from all that pollution."

Dakota and Logan chuckled, hugged Peter again and left.

Peter walked to the kitchen door leading to the party room and pushed it open. Four women stood middle of the room. He could make out Ingrid's profile. The human next to her, Fran Mitchell, smelled of yeast, sourdough, and assorted sugars. Food. The wonderous aromas that sent his pheromones howling and drooling. Following his instinct to learn how to cook, prepare those marvelous smells that tantalized his taste buds and nostrils as he prepped and made meals people raved about. Fran would be someone to coffee klatch with, exchange recipes, and buy desserts, breads, and cakes for the restaurant from. He hadn't missed the gold band on the chain around her neck. Married or spoken for. He knew that brand. The claimed mark many called it.

He, Ingrid and Fran had chatted for twenty minutes before they stepped out to check on the loud ear-piercing screeches coming from up the street. At that moment, Dakota and Logan arrived asking if he'd accidentally set off one of his alarms. The very ones they'd been testing before lunch. The new chef, Andy Kroller, showed them around the kitchen. No smoke. No burnt offerings. No issues with any of the kitchen equipment. All new. Prior equipment replaced. All alarms were off according to their panels.

Ten minutes later, Fran, Ingrid and two other women entered the party room. He stayed out of sight, observing and noting. Noting each of the new pair. The tall one next to Fran stood practically stiff. Spoke with her hands as well as her voice. She smelled of ink and paper. The odor that dust particles gave off when pages were turned, paper shuffled, and her pheromones reeked of dominance. Stubborn and full of herself. The alpha in whatever pair-bond she might be in. The female next to her. His height. Pleasing build. Meat on her bones as his grandpa used to say. Bones he wouldn't mind nibbling. Working his way up her neck, suckle her earlobe—Peter reached down and tugged his pant legs, pulling them away from his groin.

Ginger hair. The color of passion and desire. Aura flashes of yellow and red surrounded her. He inhaled twice. Deeper on the second. Magic pulsed up his nostrils and deep in his throat. Berries sweet and a hint of tartness. Pulses of energy trickling out testing, seeking, and yes! Desire and yearning. Peter stepped back from the door, swinging it quietly shut. Much more and he'd join his wolf in howling. Howling a mating call that he did not intend to let happen. Too many times attraction on all the sensual levels hit only to snap back and smack him deep in his heart. The taste was great. Eye candy was good for his wolfish desires. Acting upon those desires wasn't going to be. Pain, hurt, and cursing were not going to touch him again.

Agatha glanced over her shoulder twice. Someone watched them. Ingrid and Fran mentioned their meeting Peter. Peter G. Drake. How had she invocated Ingrid's cousin by marriage? Ingrid hadn't said Peter's name. Not even his full name. The article announcing MacGruder's sale said the new owner was P.G. Drake. Luna and the One, no mention of a complete name. Neither she nor Marjorie had researched the info further. Who and when had ignited this winning lottery event Marjorie kept calling it? Agatha stood straighter, looking around the party room. Whoever it was holding the winning lottery ticket, it sure couldn't be her.

"Agatha, are you paying attention?" Marjorie elbowed her.

"Yes, I am." Agatha moved closer to Marjorie. "Stop being a piss ant."

"Agatha, where do you think is a good place to set up the matchmaker's station?" Fran paced over to the double patio doors and back to where they stood.

"Probably along the side wall, near the doors, without blocking them. I like Ingrid's suggestion that we ask about people going out to declare their matches privately after we record them." Agatha walked over to the bar. "Long enough to line up coffee urns, hot water urns, tea bags, plus cream and sugar. Randall can dispense sodas and seltzer from one end. Kato can handle the alcohol from the other."

Fran paced off an area from the bar to the back wall to the kitchen door and back to the bar. "A hundred paces at three and a half feet per pace. Decent area for dancing. Average is nine by nine square feet per person. Most are going to be close up. A few a bit apart."

Ingrid looked down at the notes she held. "Peter says this room and the adjoining dining area are approximately nineteen thousand square feet. More than enough room for mingling, dining and dancing with you and Marjorie out of the way and in plain sight."

Marjorie shot her hand into the air as she spoke. "All in favor. Say Aye."

Fran and Ingrid's ayes followed. Agatha glanced around the room again. Her gaze lingering toward the kitchen door. Nothing felt unusual. Her taut nipples weren't at attention. The prior power surge wasn't there. The flashes of mauve and red she'd caught out of the corner of her eye were gone. Some male going through his male time of month and not bothering to damper his lust hormones. Much less his bloody damn pheromones. Last time a blast of male lust pheromones gobsmacked her, she damn near said yes to George and Lenny's let's shack up screwball proposal. She wasn't being anybody's chief cook and dishwasher, nor housekeeper while they sat back and took. Pair bond matches were partnerships no matter how many were involved.

Ingrid faced Agatha. "You in?"

"Aye." Agatha raised her hand. "Ingrid, can you and Fran oversee decorating and table layout? I need to go by Lincoln's and see what he's done. Marjorie, have we decided on event hours?"

Marjorie sighed. "We all decide event hours. Fran and Ingrid, how long do you need?"

"I'll talk to Peter tonight about his prep time and set up. Fran, what about you?" Ingrid asked.

"Cookies and rolls are done. Centerpiece cake I can do in two days. Ingrid, do you think Andy would mind helping out with the Pumpkin Sheet Cheesecakes? It'll take about twelve hours to chill and set." Fran made a note on the sheet on top of her portfolio.

"I'll ask. I think we're talking about two hours to set up and another to tear down unless Peter helps. Agatha, what do you and Marjorie need?" Ingrid glanced at her watch. "I need to go soon."

Agatha glanced at Marjorie. Marjorie shrugged. Agatha rolled her eyes. Decision was hers. "Let's go for seven to midnight. Folks can start arriving at six-thirty. If we run over, okay. Not like there's an early morning opening to worry about."

Fran raised her hand. "My aye. I'm good with that."

Ingrid raised her hand, adding her aye and buy-in.

Agatha, Fran and Ingrid stared at Marjorie.

"Okay! Okay!" Marjorie raised her hand. "Aye! I'm in."

Agatha, grinning, glanced at her watch. "I'll update Lincoln. Make sure our websites are updated. Ingrid, I'll have Lincoln check with you on..." Agatha stopped speaking. Could she say his name?

Look, Luna and the One, just because I say his name doesn't mean I'm accepting he's the one. Okay?

Agatha rubbed her ear. What was the high-pitched ringing? Why were the words we'll see echoing through her psyche?

"You'll have Lincoln check with Peter and me about updating MacGruder's website." Ingrid started toward the kitchen door. "I've got to check with Carlos and Peter on dinner. I'll talk with you later, Agatha."

"Yes, I'll let you and *Peter* know." Agatha exhaled. There, she said his name. It didn't mean anything. Right?

We'll see. Waiting is sweet and so worth it.

Agatha picked up her pace. Why were her psyche, Luna and the One being so blasted blatant about answering her invocation and prayer?

Would you prefer George and Lenny? We're only helping on what you asked help with.

Agatha stopped near Marjorie. "I've got what I need from the shop. You lock up. Talk to you later."

Agatha rushed down the alcove leading to MacGruder's main entrance. A man close to her size stood middle of her escape route. Who the hell was he? Could she slip past him?

Peter glanced up from his thoughts about placing a check-in table for the event. The woman approaching was practically running. What had her spooked? He turned, ready to help. He stopped. Running toward him was her. The one. The one he wasn't going to...

This might be the one. Remember, you asked?

Lupa on high, asking was two years ago. He'd given up on finding someone he clicked with.

Breathe deeply. You'll need her odor marking you. Ignite your pheromones and mark her as she passes.

Peter fisted his hands. He exhaled, hoping to hold his breath. No, he wasn't igniting his pheromones. Not marking anything either. He moved to the side. Getting a good look at her. Her nipples were pebbling. Crap, he'd done it anyway. Frack! Double frack! His wolf, with his tongue hanging out and panting, flashed through his conscience.

Ginger hair. Short cut. Her breasts slightly bounced as she moved. More than a handful. Nice. She stared at him momentarily as she passed. Hazel eyes? Did they flash gold as she gave him a quick once over? Her behind wasn't bad either. A bit of wiggle as she trotted past. His wolf pawed at him, whimpering and tipping his head back. Peter fisted his hands tighter. He wasn't going to mate howl. He wasn't claiming her. He was not ready for a mate. Lupa could take her blue moon intentions and cool them in several of his new chest freezers. Even his huge walk-in freezer. He was not marking and claiming a mate. Not now or any time soon.

Agatha pressed her lips together as she passed the male standing near the entrance. He wasn't bad-looking. Brindle colored hair. Neatly trimmed beard. Muscular build. Male curves in the right places. Long fingers meant—she wasn't mate shopping. Goddess, her nipples were pebbling. Was this the male who couldn't control his pheromones? Bet he dogged after a lot of women with his tongue hanging out. He could find other better looking and more available women elsewhere. Maybe *Peter* would let his employee attend the event. Find a suitable willing partner. Maybe that would keep his hot gazes elsewhere. His hot once-over blinks could tackle the women wanting and lusting.

Agatha picked up her pace again and shoved against the door handle, hurriedly opening the door. Outside she paused, inhaled, shook her hands, and glanced behind her. Why was horny dude watching her through the door? If he stepped out...she clenched her hands, ready to knock sense into the idiot. Knee him good, and—dude moved away. Good. She'd tell Ingrid about this. Poor man probably needed reminding about manners and—ringing started in her ears again. What did Luna and the One want now?

Perhaps he's the one. You did react to him. He's attracted. You noticed his physique. His looks. And wondered about other parts of his anatomy.

Not caring if his other anatomy is long or short. If he knows what to do with it, fine. The woman he chooses is sure to find out. And it ain't me.

Oh, but you could be the female.

Agatha rubbed her ear and moved on down the walk, heading for her car in the parking lot behind the shop.

Peter slowly inhaled, savoring the sweet berries and tart scent the woman gave off. It lingered. Rolling across his tastebuds and down his throat, edging its way deeper into his nethers. Rate this was going, he'd be sitting in the walk-in freezer on three cakes of ice, drinking gallons of ice water to keep from getting in over his head during the event.

He opened the door and leaned out. The chosen one, not that he had much say in it, darted across the street and into a shop called Moonlit Matches. Lupa! A matchmaker? Why a matchmaker? Peter tipped his head back, looked heavenward, sighed and went back inside MacGruder's. This was going to be a rough, different event. How did he chillax and avoid overtly ignoring his co-hosts? Steer clear of her intoxicating scent and pheromonal allure? In the same room, it wasn't going to be possible. He couldn't hide out in the kitchen all night. He snapped his fingers as he made his way back into his office from the main dining area. What he'd done with Lois might work here. Peter chuckled as he dropped into his desk chair.

Lois Auburndale, matchmaker par excellent to Hollywood's elite supernaturals and shapeshifters since the Great Reveal, had made a pass at him. First three times, he ignored her and went on about his business. Catering social events, whether the events were human ones—supernatural and magics—or even a supernatural, magics and humans mixture took him up and down the West Coast. He'd opened a few restaurants along the way. Bought and sold houses and condos as the spirit moved him or need arose. Lois had hunted him down outside San Diego in the foothills near Julian. Knocked on his door just before midnight of the autumn equinox. Claimed her car broke down. He let her stay. The stay turned into two weeks while she supposedly got her car fixed. Work kept him busy from dawn to dusk getting the old Apple Orchard Inn kitchen up to par and reopened. The Julian Bed and Breakfast claimed his attention until the night of the full moon.

Tired and ready to drop into bed, Peter got home. Shucked his clothes and showered. He made his way to his bed, ready to crawl beneath the blankets and sleep until dawn. No such luck. A feminine voice called out as he got into bed. Half-asleep or half-awake, he wasn't sure which. He leapt out of bed, partially morphed, ready to defend himself and his home. A blaze of light illuminated the room. Lois cowering on one side of the bed. Him, semi-wolfed and howling on the other. He growled as he started to morph back into human mode. Lois screamed, lurched out of the bed, and ran out of the room. By the time he'd pulled on sweatpants and a t-shirt, Lois was out the door. She tossed her belongings in her car and drove off. Later, he found out she'd planned to snare him into marrying her. She never spoke to him again. Sent him a cease and desist order. His lawyer counter filed with a clause that if she didn't sign his agreement, he would let all the California supernatural and elite know what a bogus blowhard she really was. Lois closed her business not long after she signed the agreement and left the state. Last he heard, Lois was matchmaking somewhere in Canada.

A knock on the office door roused Peter from his musings and trip down memory lane. He looked up. Carlos and Ingrid stood in the doorway. "Can we come in?"

"Sure." Peter stood. He cleared the two chairs in front of his desk. He tossed his jacket and portfolio on the desk. "Sit down. You're always welcome."

Ingrid laid her portfolio on the desk. "Fran had to go back to the bakery. Marjorie Smith and Agatha Clemons were with us. Didn't get a chance to introduce you to them."

"No worries. We'll take care of that event night, if not sooner." Peter pointed to the list on top of Ingrid's portfolio. "Food list?"

Ingrid opened her portfolio. "Minor change in menu. No steak tartare. Upped the number of roasts to twenty. Doubled the amount of au gratin potatoes and the corn and pea medley."

Peter pulled the grocery order form out of his desk. "Andy is going to call the meat order in tomorrow morning. Salad, corn, peas and potatoes are from the farmer's market. Did you get the squash handled?"

"Yes, Brisco Nells is dropping off three bushels of squash here tomorrow. Andy and his assistant take care of prepping and baking it. I'll be in tomorrow afternoon after meeting with Fran to check the ingredients needed to make the soup." Ingrid stretched. "Are you going to the house to stay or back to our place?"

"Going by the house to pick up the key from the realtor. Do a walk through at the same time. Then to your place. Be there in time for dinner." Peter tore the order sheet off and stood. "Carlos, can you stop by the market and pick up salad fixings, beef tips, and shredded cheese? I'm making a warm salad entrée for tonight."

"Sure can. What are we doing about decorations and table settings?" Carlos pulled on his jacket and took the list Peter held out.

"That is part of the meeting tomorrow with Fran and Marjorie. Agatha is handling the website updates. Have you looked at the website?" Ingrid put her portfolio in her tote and slipped her sweater on.

"Carlos, table settings are going to be white tablecloths with blue overlay. Simple, no pattern utensils. Linen napkins and the china that came with MacGruder's. White with blue trim. Fits the event theme." Peter faced Ingrid. "Website is functional. It's been getting hits. A dude named Lincoln called my website hosting service about updating graphics and linking to a ticket portal. I gave the go ahead. Marketing is a mutual cost. We'll figure it out post event. I've got enough funds from deposits and my own working capital to move forward without financial worries."

"Okay, we'll see you back at our place in a while." Carlos and Ingrid exited the office holding hands and smiling.

Peter picked up his jacket and portfolio. Two weeks ago, moving was a small hash mark on the calendar as he marked days off and completed checklists back in Los Angeles. Turning over his house keys and signing papers felt surreal. Tackling last minute changes of flying instead of driving. Waiting for his car to ship from the storage garage and passing state inspection created a lull he hadn't done more than float through. His sister and niece had kept him entertained and busy as a few family members dropped by. Even his sister agreed her face hurt from smiling so much plus gritting her teeth. Now that chapter was closed. Done and ready to consign to his past. Memories would creep up. Good ones. Bad ones. The more he moved forward embracing his here and now, the better off he might be. He still couldn't shake the feeling he was stuck between two places. Neither of them really home.

He exited his office through the kitchen, stopping to talk with Andy. "Here's the order for the meat. Get ten of each roast. Check on Thousand Island salad dressings. Going to need probably fifteen to twenty bottles unless they have gallon containers available. Get three of them. Ask about day-old bread. If they have ten loaves available, get them. I'll teach you how to make buttermilk Italian croutons with a hint of garlic and onion."

"Sounds interesting. Glad you are a hands-on owner." Andy took the list, glanced at it and added. "Do you need the ingredients for the rubs?"

"I'll pick them up in the morning. It's a personal thing picking those out." Peter waved and exited through the back door into the parking lot. He glanced around. Was the one sitting in her car waiting for him? Lupa, he hoped not.

CHAPTER FIVE
Unveiling the Past

Wednesday Morning

Peter rolled over, opened one eye and squinted. The clock on the bedside table displayed eight a.m. He'd dozed off somewhere between midnight and one. He remembered getting up once to use the bathroom. In between various dream snippets, he'd crossed into dream zone magic. The boundary that separated living from the cerebral world of dreams. He and the chosen one, Agatha as Ingrid reminded him at dinner more than once, had somehow lost their pajamas and were naked. How in the name of Lupa, his mind conjured that up, he didn't know. He wasn't going to try to figure it out either.

Evidence of his wet dream coated part of his thigh. Vivid scenes of him and Agatha touching, kissing and having sex rolled back through his subconscious as he floated back into semi-sleep.

Agatha lay beside him on her side grasping him with her hand. She stroked up and down. Slow on the downward. Tightening her hand on the upward. Squeezing as she reached his glans. Fluid leaked out, coating her hand. Agatha rubbed her palm over and around him, slicking him. Down again she stroked until she reached his testicles. Up again and back down. Faster with each stroke. He reached out, trailing his fingers down Agatha's waist, stopping as her pubic hair caressed his fingertips. He reached lower, inserting two of his fingers between her labial lips. A slight brush across Agatha's clitoris rocked her closer to him. Wetness coated his fingers. Over her clitoris with firm touches, he rubbed as more wetness flowed across his hand. Agatha pressed tighter to him. His testicles tightened to him. Peter rolled on his side as best he could. His other hand cupped Agatha's head. Their lips met.

Peter jerked awake. Vivid images flashed before him. He blinked. Inhaled slowly. Counted to ten twice and exhaled. He turned on his side. He reached out. Warmth rolled off the space next to him. Female pheromones lingered in the air. There was only one other female dream sex happened with. His high school sweetheart. Things had gone further with Agatha. They'd astral projected into each other's dreams. Bodily embraced the connection Lupa, Luna and the One were insisting on.

He tossed off the covers, shucked his briefs and hastened toward the shower. Cussing and fussing weren't going to change what happened. The connection between him and Agatha was strong. Drawing them tighter together in a web of magical connections he'd heard about but never experienced until now. How did he explain it? Magic had its own rules and science depending on the practitioner. Deity magic defied logical explanations.

Three years ago, he sold two houses in Northern California. Moved to San Diego. Revamped the Old Apple Orchard Inn. Sold homemade meals and set up a website vending business. Lois Auburn happened. Catalina Muni and her family taking on managing the inn. He dated, ventured up and down the coast. In and out of entanglements. A few short-lived romances and a broken heart or two, including his own. Losing his best friend, Mac Wolfestone, and seeing Mac laid to rest had taken more of a toll than Peter realized. Mac hadn't let on about his health.

Mac had been a cornerstone to the businesses they built together. A foundation centerpiece to their mutual relationship with Penny Goldsmith. Penny's decision to move away had surprised Mac and him more than either of them understood until Mac bared his soul before he left for Europe.

Peter turned on the shower and stepped in. He picked up the soap and worked up a lather between his hands. More memories came flooding back as he washed and rinsed.

He procrastinated starting over in one spot as he moved up and down the coast taking various chef jobs. Helping friends out with their restaurants. Selling the Old Apple Orchard Inn to Catalina and her family was a high point in the last year. They took the inn from a local restaurant to a local tourist destination. He sold his last remaining share in the inn to Catalina right before he left. She kept refusing to accept the buyout without paying him. He quietly deeded the property to her, paying the property taxes out of what she'd paid him for the share he sold her.

Peter shut off the shower, stepped out on the bath mat, and glanced in the mirror. A few gray hairs dotted his head in places. Worry, stress, and illness from time to time his physician reassured him. It wasn't the gray that bothered him. It was being single. Alone and without a pack to call home. Carlos and Ingrid were part of the few blood family he could count on welcoming him. Embracing who he was, is, and had potential to become. With a mate by his side, working toward another successful local restaurant launch that fed Cauldron Falls and Sylvan Valley and the few other magic and supernatural enclaves close-by made it worthwhile. As more humans and supernaturals understood each other, embraced their diversities and learned how to build a wonderful life for each other, success wasn't about being internationally known or even nationally known. It was locally known, trusted, and integrated into the fabric of everyday life that made up Cauldron Falls and Sylvan Valley.

He toweled off, hung the damp towel up, and exited the bathroom. A lone thought slid across his mind as he tossed clothes on the bed. Had their astral projection mating affected Agatha the same way it had him?

Agatha wrapped her quilted comforter around her tighter. She chafed her hands again as a new set of shivers rippled over her. The brindle-haired one's thoughts echoed through her mind, calling her his, marking her with his words and essence. In the second dream, they lay side by side, nude, and touching in intimate ways. Stroking. Caressing. Building heat and desire until both of them climaxed. Praise Luna, he hadn't slid into her. Dream impregnation was not where she ever wanted to venture.

Astral projection sex and dream impregnation bonded the couple together in ways that most matchmakers dared not talk about, mention, or dabble in understanding. A few of the ancient tomes housed in the SH&M's central vault described the cause and effects of dream magic and the ban on practicing such. Agatha chafed her arms and hands vigorously. Praise the One, all witch matchmakers, female and male, oaths included a vow against dabbling in ancient magic. Better left to those that came before. Left to Lupa, Luna and the One, and personal deities. Magic lost in translation could unleash things far worse than chaos and return things to prior to the Great Reveal. Not a place she ever wanted to dream about, visit, or think about.

Agatha shoved the comforter off and stood. She stretched. Marjorie had teased her about not meeting Peter. Not asking about a picture of him. Marjorie accused her of avoiding him. Agatha tossed her sleep shirt in the hamper. She tested the shower warmth and stepped under the spray. She worked shower gel into the sea sponge, lathered her body, and rinsed. Washing her hair took a few more minutes. She wrapped her hair in a towel, pulled her terrycloth bathrobe on and exited the bathroom. She sat in the wingback chair in the corner of her room next to the east-facing window. Watching the morning sunrise offered her a few moments of peace and quiet. Time to reflect on the previous day and prepare for the current one.

Joel McGowen, a former beau, taught her the beauty of the moment. The moments watching the sunset painting bold, lush, colorful strokes across the sky welcoming the night sky full of stars and even more wonders. The quiet lulls as the sun first peaked across the horizon heralding a new day. A new beginning. A new start and a reason to continue being, growing and learning. The stories he told his children, nieces and nephews, and his students enthralled all who heard them. Listened to his intonations and storytelling talent. Joel's last letter contained pictures of his grandnieces. He had found happiness with Merle. Agatha smiled thinking about the joy his voice carried the last time they talked.

She opened her portfolio and pulled out the printouts of the last two emails from Lincoln and his schematics for the website updates.

A muted full moon outlined in blue was the backdrop for the white, red, and yellow lettering announcing the event. Lincoln had tweaked the wording a bit. He hadn't gone with the gothic lettering one of his graphics artists had suggested. The large fat font filled with either white, red or yellow stood out. Each section grabbed attention. The location time and place in a medium blue against a white starburst shadowed background made sure no one missed the vital information or the click here to purchase tickets. Agatha nodded. Lincoln had captured the message, meaning and subtle messages without overshadowing any pertinent information. He repeated the background from the website event page to the ticket portal. White blocks showed where information needed to be entered and forms of payment accepted. She'd given Lincoln the go-ahead on processing the updates.

Marjorie had blown up her phone with text messages and calls until almost midnight about the updates and activated the ticket portal. Agatha had sent everything to voice mail or muted it all but emergency contact numbers. Curling up in bed with the latest cozy mystery by a childhood friend had capped her evening and lulled her to sleep.

Agatha glanced at the clock on her nightstand. Nine-thirty. She had plenty of time to relax and not think about brindle hair or Peter G. Drake. Her mind had wandered down memory lane in her moments awake during the night. Old relationships popped up. Men who needed to grow up. Men who still acted like boys at twenty-one. Men who wanted submission and them put on a pedestal. Agatha smiled.

Tony Muson had tried more than once to get her to agree to his ideal relationship. She saw only him while he got to run around and collect admirers and procreate. Problem was Tony didn't get that he was zip in both of his procreate and admirers collection.

She laid her portfolio on the bed. Her memory lane walk continued as she picked out her clothes. Zachary Stillwell was a sweetie. He'd hung around even after they'd decided that living under the same roof just didn't work. Zachary loved his freedom. Loved to stay up all night and sleep most of the day. His night owl habits weren't a big issue. His snoring was. Shapeshifter bears tended to snore especially during bouts of deep sleep. Zachary looked her up every time he and his pride came to town. His two wives and seven children were gems. Smiles and laughter multiplied with their visits.

Samuel Ponce was one of the three that got the closest. They'd got halfway through their second thirty-day full moon match when all hades let loose. His family didn't like her looks, her genetics, or her lineage. No magic royalty. No distinctive magic traits. Not one drop of shapeshifter blood. Samuel's family was a proverbial blend of lineages, magics, plus bits and pieces of different shapeshifter traits. Agatha smiled remembering Samuel telling his family patriarch and maternal grandmother his secret. Catching his family off-guard and revealing his two husbands had shut up the tirades that had been going on for over an hour that night. Samuel asked for his moon match ring back in front of his family and thanked her for being the witness to his and his husbands' moonlight marriages. Samuel, his two husbands, and she had thrown their families off their insistent matchmaking attempts and ongoing lectures about settling down.

Rob Nicely still made her shake her head and wonder if she knew her heart. They'd dated in high school. His first year of junior college. He even gave her a promise ring. What he promised and what she thought the promise was were two distinctly different things. Rob promised he'd return to Cauldron Falls. He kept that part of the promise. He also promised to pick up where they left off if he returned and silently muttered 'if he felt the same way'. Agatha knuckled a tear off her cheek. Rob had been her first in many ways. Her first physical lover. Her first time in love. Falling deeper than she'd ever done before. Rob called her beautiful. Complemented her lavishly. Gifted her with experience. Experience learning to watch what a man said. The more a guy praised and swooned to quote him, the more she stayed way, far away. Avoiding involvement.

Agatha pulled on jeans and a loose-knit top. She sat on the bed, putting on socks and her sneakers as she continued reminiscing. The man who got the trophy for her swearing-off full moon matches was Tristan Moorefield. Scoundrel extraordinaire. Bastard wanted her to give up her magic, forsake her calling and work to pay off his bills. Not *her* bills or *their* bills. *His* bills. He pushed for joint bank accounts and wanted to know where, when, and why she spent any money. He tried to take over her business. Alienated Marjorie to the point Marjorie almost walked away from their long time friendship. Last she heard, Tristan had eloped with a lesser-known royal magic to some small principality in Europe. Probably working as a stable hand. Good job for him, given his asinine attitude. Mules belonged in barns with others of their kind.

Agatha stood, straightened her bed, picked up her portfolio and fanny pack. As she made her way through the living room toward the kitchen, she glanced out the window noting where the morning paper lay on the driveway. Clouds littered the sky blocking out part of the sun. Fall colors peppered a few of the leaves of the oak tree across the street. Two of her neighbors and their dogs walked past. The peaceful, family-accepting ambiance of the neighborhood exemplified what Cauldron Falls and Sylvan Valley had become and worked to remain. Accepting, embracing, and welcoming diversity. She walked into the kitchen, plugged the coffeemaker in, and put her fanny pack and portfolio on the table. She hoped her delivery milkman remembered the scones she'd added to her order last night. Fresh yogurt, berries and scones plus fresh churned cream. Efrim and Rhoda knew everyone's preferences on their delivery route. Texting them allowed for adding to an order. Rural living with city mix. Big city living wasn't where she wanted to live.

Thirty minutes later, Agatha pulled out of her driveway. She'd stopped long enough to pick up the paper. Her second mug of tea filled her commuter mug. The twenty-minute drive into town might be that long. Rush hour traffic didn't exist. Oldies folk rock poured out of the radio as she drove. She knew one thing as she pulled into the parking lot behind Moonlit Matches. Whether her gut said no or not, her psyche and mind said she had to see a picture of Peter G. Drake. Also, get brindle-hair's name. She needed to put distance between her and him. Maybe she could talk to Peter and they could work out a fake interest for the event. Have a few friendly dates. Her help him get to know folks. Him help her keep her secret without her telling him about it. Mutual benefit to her way of thinking.

Voices greeted Agatha as she entered the shop through the back door. Marjorie's car was in its usual spot. Fran and Ingrid were busy sorting the decorations Siobhan had dropped off and deciding what else to add from Fran's Halloween decorations. No meetings were on the agenda according to the online planner she and Marjorie shared.

"I think you're on to something with that idea." Marjorie walked around her desk.

"Ingrid mentioned you and Agatha could fill me in on the matchmaker traditions." Brindle-hair followed Marjorie toward the hall.

"Sure can, Peter." Marjorie stopped partway into the hall. "I think I saw Agatha pull into the parking lot. Let me check. I've got a couple of brochures in the back that can help with the explanation."

Agatha halted. Brindle-hair? Peter? No. Agatha slowly turned. Goddess above, how more obvious could Luna and the One get? Agatha took two steps forward.

"Agatha, where you going?" Marjorie called out. "Forget something?"

Agatha caught her top lip between her teeth, stifling her first response. She gripped her tote tighter and turned. "No, didn't forget anything."

"Good. There's someone who wants to meet you." Marjorie motioned her forward as she picked up two of their brochures off the shelf close to the back room entrance.

"Yes, I'm interested in meeting Agatha." Peter stepped around Marjorie, halting abruptly.

Agatha nodded, trying to shield. Envisioning a barrier around her took thought she couldn't muster. Reds, yellows, and mauves flashed around Peter. Arcing out toward her in bold repetitive bursts. Could she shake his hand? Clasp his hand and let go?

"Pleasure to meet you." Agatha stepped forward, holding her hand out.

Peter swallowed twice, glanced at Marjorie, and back to Agatha. It was her. She was the one? The chosen? Lupa, could he be in the same room and not...His wolf tipped his head back and let out an enormous howl. One after another. Peter clenched his hands, trying to hush his wolf. Peter glanced down, willing his groin to behave and not be rigid with lustful interest.

Peter looked up. Agatha approached with a hand out. Could he touch her and remain aloof?

"Good to put a face and name together." Peter took a step forward. He inhaled twice, focusing on the hand in front of him. The first touch of the one. The chosen one for him.

Agatha moved closer to him. She started to lower her hand.

Marjorie stepped between them. "You two go on out front. I'll make tea and bring out some cookies."

Peter blinked and nodded. "Yes, an afternoon snack sounds awesome."

He turned and walked back into the shop. He reached down, adjusting the crotch of his pants, willing his wolf to silence. He snuck a quick glance back as he rounded the first desk. Agatha snatched the brochures Marjorie held, shook her head, and let go what looked like a deep sigh. Her breasts rose and fell with each breath she took. Peter closed his eyes, tapped his fingers against his leg, and opened his eyes. He sat in the chair furthest from the desk. Keeping his mind on business was going to take a lot of concentration.

Agatha paused at the edge of the hallway before entering the shop. Peter G. Drake sat at her desk. He matched her height. Muscular. Neatly trimmed beard and mustache. Her nipples started to tighten. He wasn't hard on the eyes. Brindle-haired had a name. A voice. A personality. Business Agatha. Focus on business. Business, not the luscious dream intimacy they shared. Peter had had the same dream, right?

CHAPTER SIX

A Bewitching Encounter

Wednesday Afternoon

Agatha set her tote on her desk. "Peter, Marjorie says you want to know about Cauldron Falls Sadie Hawkins events."

"Understanding my new home community and the business practices makes a lot of sense, don't you think?" Peter pointed to a wreath of flowers hanging on the shelf close to the register. "Lilac symbolizes flirtation, attraction, and possible short courtship."

"Are you flirting with me?" Agatha pulled out her desk chair and sat in it.

"If you want me to, I can." Peter grinned and winked at her.

Agatha looked away. Where was Marjorie with the tea and cookies?

"We're focusing on business." Agatha pointed to other flower arrangements and items in the shop. "Nature plays a part in magic. I'm sure you know that. We sell a number of items related to practical magic, personal magic, and our main business, matchmaking."

"Do you make many matches outside of these full moon events?" Peter shifted in his chair, facing her more.

"Yes. Matchmaking is an essential part of the supernatural and magic communities. Especially since the Great Reveal. More humans are moving into our communities. They're embracing our ways and traditions. Some are eager to find a mate." Agatha tapped the brochure. "Sadie Hawkins is a unique part of Cauldron Falls and Sylvan Valley."

"Sadie Hawkins is the women ask the men." Peter opened the brochure, making sure he didn't touch Agatha's hand or fingers. "More women than men?"

Agatha shook her head. "Population ebbs and flows both ways. First Sadie Hawkins event was conceived by Lisa Hendricks and Tasha

Cauldron, the wives of Cauldron Falls and Sylvan Valley's founders. Getting people to mingle and mix was the objective."

Peter nodded. "When did full moon matches enter?"

Marjorie laughed as she set the tray with cookies and mugs of tea on the desk. "When more single women than men started showing up."

Agatha glared at Marjorie. "Not quite. Arranged marriages were part of traditions many magics brought from the old countries. Some supernaturals feared rejection. Letting women lead often broke the ice."

"Like setting yourself up rather than someone else doing it or blind dating without seeing the person first or possibly knowing a bit about the other attendees." Peter nodded. "Makes sense."

Marjorie sat in the chair next to Peter. "After the Great Reveal, magic became commonplace. Supernaturals, magics, and humans started letting down their guard. Full moons allowed people to stay out longer and more mingling happening."

"City council and the mayors of both towns decreed Sadie Hawkins Full Moon events an ongoing part of civic functions. We matchmakers got involved when people wanted to record their match choices or some marriages take place during the event." Agatha reached for the brochure. Her hand brushed against Peter's. Flashes of lilac, mauve and orange outlined their hands and vanished.

"Did you see that?" Peter drew his hand back.

Marjorie hastily finished her tea and cookie. "I've got an appointment. Prenup discussion number two."

Agatha stood. "You didn't mention it. It's not on the planner."

"Got the call on my way in." Marjorie set her mug on the tray. "You two keep talking. I'll be back before closing."

Marjorie retrieved her tote from the back room, waving as she exited the front door of the shop.

Peter watched the shop door close. He leaned forward, placing his hand near Agatha's. "Something is happening between us. You're gonna tell me you didn't see the sparks?"

Agatha started to pull her hand back. Peter laid his hand on top of Agatha's. More sparks filled the air. Spurts of reds, yellows, and mauves outlined their hands and continued up their arms until a hazy aura outlined Peter.

"Do you see sparks?" Agatha gripped part of her top in her free hand below the desk, out of sight. She knew Carlos and Ingrid were shapeshifters. Neither had said if Peter was supernatural, magic, or human. A few magic and supernatural traits skipped offspring from time to time.

Peter sluggishly slid his hand off Agatha's. Registered matchmakers were witches. The Matchmakers' Council seal of approval logo was on the door. Registered matchmaker logo next to it. Why was Agatha avoiding answering his questions? He wet his lips and asked, "Are you avoiding me?"

Agatha pulled back, shot him a quizzical look and shook her head. "What makes you think that?"

"I asked if you saw sparks. You countered with a question." Peter rose and rounded the desk. "I've touched you twice. Colored aura blasts and aura sparks."

"Might of been a few." Agatha pushed her chair back from the desk.

Peter advanced, closing the space between them. "You're going to deny our astral projection mating and the dream sex, too?"

Agatha jumped out of her chair, shoving it between her and Peter. "Back off!"

"I'm sorry." Peter moved back, stopping at the corner of the desk. "My wolf and I smell your feminine response to our pheromones. You're attracted. I'm attracted."

Agatha stared at Peter. Peter held out his hand. "Yes, I'm a wolf shifter. Wolves know their mates by smell. I've smelled mine. It's you. Thanks for the information. See you at the event."

Peter walked out the shop's front door, didn't look back, and crossed the street.

Agatha swiped her hands down her jeans twice. She laid her palms against the desk, breathing deeply. Sparks floated in the air. Blues, reds and greens. Lust and desire aura colors. She closed her eyes hoping the sparks stopped. Instead, words flashed through her psyche. *You're his mate. He's your mate. You asked. We answered. Stop denying what each of you wants.*

A wolf howl echoed and ceased as she opened her eyes. Agatha dropped into her chair, covering her face with her hands. No man beyond Rob had ever affected her this way. She'd flirted, shared a few kisses and some nude cuddles. Not astral projection and dream mating. She needed time to think. Time to understand why this frightened her. Why had she doubted so much? There was a time she embraced taking chances. Embraced her attractiveness and comfort in her own being. When had that changed? Three rejections ago? When Rob returned?

Agatha lowered her hands. She pulled the mirror out of her tote bag. When was the last time she'd looked in the mirror and admired herself? Not in a vain way. Admired herself care. Her concern for her wellbeing. Time had come to focus on what she wanted and needed. Her best friend, self, and a mate. Luna, had she found him? Or was it he found her?

Peter didn't stop until he reached MacGruder's front door. Had he made a pass at Agatha? Blurted out his attraction? His wolf sat on his haunches, grinning and wagging his tail. "Some help you are. Spraying pheromones. Except you hope to mark and claim. Not scare off like a spooked skunk!"

Agatha's feminine fertility hormones reached out, lured him closer, and smacked him. Smacked his male ego and horny libido to the point he wanted to pull her to him and kiss her until both of them surrendered. Surrendered to the desire and lust smoking around them. Their aura sparks were sizzling and setting off more sparks. He could smell all of it. Marking and claiming her was subliminal compared to what his subconscious kept screaming at him. *Don't do it!*

Peter unlocked MacGruder's door, entered and locked the door behind him. He wasn't backing out on the event. Business deals mattered. That was his focus. Not Agatha. He'd deal with him and her later.

He entered the kitchen. Andy waved him at him. "Peter, need to talk with you."

"Sure, what's up?" Peter threaded his way through the kitchen to the prep table where Andy stood.

"Meat order is in. If we're going to marinade the roasts, need to get it going today. Slow roasting them is going to take most of the day Saturday. Unless I come in early."

"I'll get the rub going. The marinade is an easy recipe. I'll have it for you in a moment. Need to get it out of my office. No double shifts. We'll talk more about that later." Peter made his way to his office. Saturday was going to be a full day of cooking, entertaining, and inhaling more of his sweet Agatha's pheromones and hormones. Could he withstand the heat of the kitchen and his libido?

He shucked his sweaty t-shirt and tossed it on the desk. Took one of his spare white t-shirts out of the wardrobe next to the desk and put it on. Pulled on his favorite chef jacket and rubbed his hands together. Marinade recipe choice. Which one? The Hollywood Love Potion? Two-thirds cup red wine, smidgen of oregano, basil, seasoned salt and enough rose water to finish covering the roast. Add a few jalapenos and sugar to give it a heat that slid across the tongue and down the throat, warming the heart as it made its way to the stomach. Northern California Hots? Tobasco, fermented wine, two dark beers, and cloves plus brown sugar and garlic with a hint of onion. Blue moon...Peter clapped his hands. He knew which marinade and rub he was making. Blue Lagoon Honeymoon.

He flipped his recipe binder open, flipping page protectors until he found what he looked for. Blue Lagoon Honeymoon Marinade and Rub. Rub consisted of three cups brown sugar, a pinch of dried red

MOONLIT MATCH

chili peppers, two banana peppers deseeded and diced, plus minced purple onion, lemon juice, and lime juice. Once the rub was applied, he'd dowse the meat with a partly fermented California blush wine. Let the rub and wine soak for ten to twelve hours. Permeate the meat, tenderizing and imbuing all the spice flavors. Marinade was simple repeat of the rub diluted with more of the blush wine and added red wine mid-way through the three-hour process. Tender roast. Slightly drunk if anyone measured the roast's alcohol level. Honey rub prior to roasting the spitted roasts slowly in a three hundred-and-fifty-degree oven for about four hours. If the roast got dry, spritz with more of the marinade.

Peter joined Andy at the prep table. He laid the recipe on the table. "Here's what we're going to make. You get the ingredients while I trim the fat off the roasts and tie them up."

Andy grinned. "Tying things up in cooking has always been a high point. High in that you get to practice your shifter scout knots without having to worry about what you're tying up getting away."

Peter chortled. "Yeah. One scoutmaster had us practice our knots on each other. Problem was some of us figured the tighter the knot, the better it was. We dulled a pair of garden scissors that outing in one afternoon."

Andy walked away, laughing loudly. "I'll get the ingredients. Be right back."

Peter put on a double set of prep gloves. He set three roasts on the prep table. He trimmed the fat off each, wrapped twine around them, and returned them to the walk-in. He set several more roasts on the table and repeated his preparations. Each roast was alone. Stood on its own merits. It was a part of the whole prior to butcher preparation. Peter laid down the serrated knife he held.

Standing on his own had become a remote part of him. He didn't think twice about going home alone. Waking up alone. Until now. Had he given up on losing the emptiness he felt deep inside? The loneliness that snuck up on him more obviously in the last few months than before. Had he stopped dwelling on what was supposed to be according to all the biological studies and latest mating scientific studies? Was this the time and place to embrace love again? Take a chance on dating, finding someone to care about? Build a future with?

Andy placed two mixing bowls on the clear end of the prep table. "Three cups of brown sugar in each. A pinch of dried red chili peppers and two pinches of dried smoked paprika for a little extra oomph. I grated and juiced a whole lemon and lime in each bowl. Still need two banana peppers deseeded and diced, plus minced purple onion."

"Great job and improvising for an extra flavor punch. Blue Lagoon Honeymoon came from an impromptu seasoning mix for a barbeque that a friend and I got invited to. His best friend's cousin wanted the recipe and what the rub was called. Beach front barbecue party next to a lagoon, thus the name. Honeymoon came from someone shouting out the word." Peter returned the prepped roasts to the walk-in. He wiped down and sanitized the table. "Get the large wooden chopping board and the smaller synthetic one. I'll grab the gloves we need for handling the peppers."

Andy laid the two chopping boards on the prep table along with two small carving knives. He laid double layers of parchment paper on the synthetic board. "Handling onions and banana peppers requires gloves for sure."

Peter chuckled. He took off his gloves from trimming the roasts. "Helps keep the sting down, and the smell. When its time to do the rub, a new pair of gloves. With as many roasts as we're doing, possibly will change gloves partway through."

"Duly noted. I'll get the banana peppers and onions. How many of each?" Andy set a box of prep gloves on the table.

"Grab the two jars of banana peppers out of the walk-in and four large onions." Peter put on a new pair of gloves and pulled the parchment paper and synthetic chopping board to him.

The next ten minutes his and Andy's eyes watered, sniffles happened, plus laughter and teamwork. Peter stripped off his gloves and tossed them in the trash receptacle near the back door. "Make sure that trash bag goes out tonight. In fact, I'll take it out when we're done with rubbing down the roasts and soaking them with the fermented wine."

Andy tossed his gloves in the receptacle. "Good thing I put two large hand soap containers on the sink. This smell is reeking and gonna take triple hand washing."

Peter chuckled. "Yeah. Be thankful I told you about the gloves. It took me and my pal two weeks to get the smell off our hands. The pepper juice was gone. Thank Lupa for that! Or washing certain body parts would have been very, very interesting."

Andy sputtered and snickered. "Oh, I bet. First time I minced onion and jalapenos together, I learned no deep breaths. I sounded like I'd been on a ten-day crying jag and my eyes looked like it too."

Thirty minutes later, ten of the roasts were rubbed, soaking in wine, and sitting side by side on the same shelf. Peter pulled off his third pair of gloves. He wiped his forehead with his sleeve. "Andy, I'm leaving the rest of the roast rubbing and drunking to you. I'm going over to Mitchell's to grab us a couple of sandwiches and sweets. I'll be back in a bit."

Peter entered his office, took off his chef jacket, tossed it in the hamper holding the rest of the laundry the linen service would pick up tomorrow when they delivered the table cloths and napkins for Saturday night. He donned his jacket, zipped it up and grabbed his t-shirt off his desk. He waved to Andy as he exited via the back door. Peter trotted down the loading dock steps, stopping at his car long enough to toss his shirt inside. As he relocked the car, he gazed out over the parking lot. Parking capacity was a hundred cars. Saturday night RSVPs were at sixty with more in the portal when he checked with Lincoln. Praise Lupa, only paid RSVPs were getting through. Lincoln said the plus and minus factor was seven to twelve more. Odd number in case some people didn't make it. Refunds were on a case by case basis. Cancellation deadline was Thursday noon. Parking wasn't a problem. Carlos had hired a neighbor's two sons, looking to make extra money, to oversee valet services. Keys would be turned in to the coat room attendant for safekeeping.

Peter walked down the driveway separating MacGruder's and the four-story office building going up next door. Daytime parking would take up part of MacGruder's parking lot. Building tenants would pay for the spaces on a monthly basis. His business investment was paying off. Now if he could get his personal life settled, things might be rosy most of the time. Except in the spring when his blasted hay fever and allergies kicked up.

He paused at the shop next to Mitchell's. A new florist grand opening. No one had mentioned Saturday night's table centerpieces. He'd see what they had to offer. A bouquet of lilacs and mauve tulips tied with a red bow for a certain someone wouldn't hurt.

"Hi, Fran," Peter called out as he walked into Mitchell's. "How's business?"

"Hey, Peter," Fran replied, exiting the kitchen, wiping her hands on a towel. "Busy and lulls in spurts. How's things?"

"Busy with prep for Saturday night." Peter tapped the counter case. "I'll take two of the beef, ham and gouda cheese sandwiches. A dozen of your freshest cookies. And..."

Peter walked over to the wedding cake display case. "Got a couple of cookies you can do a bit of writing on for me? Keep the writing between us?"

"Do you want to decorate them yourself and box them up?" Fran slid open the display case door. "Which ones do you want?"

Peter squatted down, looking at both rows of cookies and small cakes meant for the top tier of wedding cakes. Two different ones caught his eye as he figured out what he wanted to say on the cookies.

"The two with the red and white on them. I'll do the decorating when I get back. I'm going next door to the florist."

"Glad you are. That's the shop we're using for the centerpieces." Fran took the two cookies out. "I'll have your sandwiches and mixed dozen of the cookies ready when you get back."

Peter shot Fran two thumbs up and exited the bakery. He paused outside the floral shop looking at the arrangements in the window along with the vases containing bouquets outside near the shop entrance. The shop door opened. A middle-aged woman stepped out. "Can I help you?"

Peter faced the woman. "Good afternoon. I'm Peter Drake. MacGruder's new owner."

"Janet Staxon." Janet shook Peter's hand. "I heard about MacGruder's expanding and a new owner. Nice to meet you."

"Thanks. I'm checking on the floral arrangements for Saturday night's event." Peter grabbed a bouquet out of one of the vases. "I want these, too."

Janet started back into the shop. "Sure. Come on in. Let me see what's on the order for Saturday."

Peter glanced left and right as he entered the shop. One side held potted plants and artificial floral displays. On the opposite were refrigerated units with sliding doors holding vases of cut flowers and a shelf displaying arrangements. On the shelves next to the refrigerated units were small potted scenic plants display. He grinned, pointing to one. "I had one like that on my desk in my San Diego office. Gift from my staff on my first birthday with them."

"Did you just move to Cauldron Falls?" Janet took the particular potted display off the shelf.

"Finished building a house out toward Cauldron Way. Staying with my cousins Carlos and Ingrid." Peter flexed one hand. He told her more in the five minutes since Janet and he introduced themselves. Networking with fellow merchants and business folks meant spilling bits and pieces about yourself. He usually stuck to business. Why he added about the house he didn't know.

"Great area for building. Lots of room for gardens, privacy, and room to let your hair down from time to time." Janet winked and reached for the bouquet he held. "I can wrap these up for you. I'm gifting you the desk planter. A way to remember where you came from and why you moved here."

Peter pressed his lips against each other. How was Janet reading him?

Janet rolled clear wrap out on the counter. "Ingrid and I are good friends. She mentioned you wanted a place with room to meander at will. May your full moon shifts be pleasant."

Janet handed him the flowers as she continued speaking. "Table centerpieces are a white vase with two flowers and a sprig of myrtle fronds. Flowers are Moonlight lilies and deep red carnations. Hint of color, moonlight, and magic."

"Sounds great. Similar for the other event arrangements?" Peter pulled his wallet out.

"Yes." Janet rang up Peter's purchase. She wrapped a vase and put it in a box on the counter. "Last one left. You can have it free of charge. Will go great with the bouquet."

"Thank you. Appreciate the business and vase." Peter laid what he owed on the counter along with his business card. "I'm doing catering, too. If you or someone you know needs catering, give me a call."

Janet placed his business card in the rolodex on the counter near the phone. "Awesome. Drop by again."

Peter waved as he exited. Business connection. Another item checked off the list he had from Ingrid, Fran, and Marjorie plus his delicious Agatha. He swallowed hard as he entered Mitchell's. Last time he had it this bad, he'd almost gotten engaged and hitched. If this was the result of one astral projection sex session, what if he touched more than her hand? Kissed her? Even held her close?

CHAPTER SEVEN

Magic in the Air

Thursday Evening

    Peter exited the shower, grabbed the towel off the counter and began drying. His first shower in his new home. His favorite towel and soap were in place. He inhaled deeply. Smells of fresh air greeted him. Open windows and the evening breeze filtered in, carrying with it scents of damp earth, decomposing leaves and the crisp chill that signaled mid-fall was arriving. An old business acquaintance had called while the movers were unpacking and placing his furniture. A day earlier than expected. Definitely a blessing that let him take part of the worries he carried off his shoulders. Check moving off his list. Carlos had helped with the boxes that needed immediate unpacking. Ingrid made a grocery and staples run. Food, internet, cable TV and phone were working. Ingrid had teased him about making a home cooked meal for one. He faked his responses well. Carlos and Ingrid left thinking he wanted his first night in his new home alone. Time to settle in and decompress.

    He hung his towel on the heated towel rack. One luxury that he didn't spare money on. Solar panels showed full capacity and working fine as he went from room to room turning lights on after the movers, Carlos and Ingrid left. Dressing for the evening took his focus in another direction. Peter tossed a deep lilac-colored shirt on the bed, jeans and underwear. He quickly dressed, brushed his hair and beard, slipped his shoes on and moved into the living room. His jacket lay on the chair close to the front door. The garage would take another week to finish.

Parking his car in his own driveway had surprised him more than he admitted out loud. The first place he owned was a condo with off-street parking. In California, he didn't have weather to worry about. Climate change necessitated garages and parking under cover. He was glad he wasn't paying West Coast prices for anything. He didn't have to be thrifty. He chose to be thrifty. Moving, starting a new business without having to invest a lot of overhead and drum up clientele was worth the time and energy.

Time to move into a new phase of being. His dreams last night had him awake at different intervals. Pondering what they meant. Close to dawn, he dreamt of her again. The one that he still didn't understand. The one that baffled him in the moments he stopped focusing on the event and business.

Peter stretched as he entered the kitchen. Fresh coffee smells greeted him. He filled a mug with freshly brewed decaf, sugar cookie-flavored coffee. He pulled out the chair closest to him and sat at the kitchen table. A small bowl of warmed chili awaited his tastebuds. Leftovers from the hasty thrown together luncheon Andy had concocted for all the staff and new hires. Peter tossed a hand full of oyster crackers into the chili and stirred. He took a small bite waiting for the heat of the diced jalapenos and banana peppers to waltz slowly across his tastebuds, followed by the tart sweetness of the leftover fermented wine from the marinade. As he ate, Peter went back over the employee luncheon.

Pep talks and understanding about Saturday night were eagerly met. A few of the returning staff stayed, helping Andy set up the party room table and chairs. Three of the more tenured staff offered to help out in the kitchen with Saturday evening's preparations. Keeping food rolling, clean up happening, and staff fed. Each of the three knew from former Sadie Hawkins events they found their matches at that planning and staging helped to a point. This event, being smaller and more intimate, was going to need less directional leadership. That meant he could mingle and talk with his guests. See the event as it happened.

Peter drank the remaining third of his coffee and pushed back from the table. He rinsed his bowl, spoon, and mug and placed them in the dishwasher. He emptied the coffee maker and turned it off. Iced decaf would await him for the morning. Great pick me up as he drove to work.

He pulled his jacket on, closed the windows, set the alarm system and exited the house carrying the box from Staxon's and the bouquet. He laid the box holding the vase and, the two cookies from Mitchell's and the bouquet on the passenger's seat. Peter looked at the house, smiled and started the car. Fifteen forty-two Cauldron Way was officially his. He was definitely settling into being home.

Agatha pushed the calculator and bank statements across her desk. Marjorie had left early to pick Terrence up at the Nashville airport. They would be back tomorrow mid-morning. The late evening flight gave Marjorie and Terrence time to catch up over dinner at one of their fave Nashville restaurants and an overnight without worrying about rush hour traffic.

Marjorie had stopped needling her about Peter. Since meeting him, Agatha had taken care to avoid in person meetings. Phone calls and email worked fine. Getting too close and the zapping started. He'd touched her and she sizzled for forty-eight hours. Her psyche still drummed up the feeling in the middle of the night awakening her from dreamless sleep to toss her back into the astral projection sex dream replayed.

Agatha stood and stretched. The wall clock above the shop door showed twenty minutes until closing. Twenty minutes to contemplate where she would get a takeout dinner and what movie she would watch while she ate. She picked up the checkbook and bank statements, put them in the filing cabinet and locked the cabinet. Marjorie had balanced the register's cash totals and made the bank deposit on her way out of town. Locking the register, signing off the credit card terminal and flipping the open sign to shut was all that remained. Getting last minute customers rarely happened. Agatha stepped outside the shop door, shielding her eyes, looking at the start of the evening's sunset. Streaks of orange, purple and fragments of blue sky illuminated the sky. A few stray clouds moved along the horizon.

"Nice evening."

Agatha lowered her hand, turned around, and entered the shop muttering. "He couldn't leave well enough be. Had to show up. Drop by. Hopefully on his way home. Letting me close up in peace and quiet."

"Had to show up, yes." Peter followed her inside the shop. "On my way home, no. Here to see you, for sure."

Peter leaned against the counter. He held a box entwined with a red and white ribbon in one hand. His hand covered part of the lettering on the box. In his other was a bouquet of fall-colored flowers. Vibrant oranges, yellows and in the center were... Agatha tried to glance away. The center flowers matched his—crap. Peter G. Drake wore a flirting color and the dang bouquet had lilacs practically dead center. He had to be kidding, right?

Agatha opened her mouth. Words failed her. She pointed at Peter and the bouquet. She shook her head, backing away. Peter moved forward, nodding.

"Yes, you. Yes, flirtation. *And...* " Peter stopped speaking.

Agatha shook her head more. She held her hands up. "Not flirting with me."

"Got your attention. Good." Peter moved two steps closer. "Maybe we're beyond flirting."

"*Oh?*" Agatha grimaced at her emphasis. She sounded like she was turned on. Experiencing hormonal and pheromonal ecstasy simultaneously. She couldn't be, could she?

"Like your response." Peter grinned and sat in a chair in front of her desk.

Agatha moved behind her desk. "What do you want?"

Peter leaned forward. "Have dinner with me. Talk about this attraction. Figure out what we're going to do about it."

"Dinner? You and me? Alone?" Agatha dropped into her desk chair. "I don't think..."

"Stop." Peter held up a hand. "Thinking is what we need to do. Together, to figure out what is going on."

Agatha shoved hard against the desk, propelling her and the chair backwards.

Peter rushed around the desk as Agatha stood, rocking forward. He clasped her arm, steadying her. Heat, intense heat shot through his palm, crackled up his arm, stopping at his shoulders. His beard puffed out. He could feel the hair on his head mimicking his beard. Sparks crackled and flashed. Peter reached out with his other hand steadying Agatha as she reached for the desk. She toddled toward him, trying to speak. Her hair puffed out like his with small sparks emitting from different places. He pulled her toward him as he turned resting his hips against the desk, hoping to steady both of them and ground the electrical magnetism they'd set off.

Agatha stumbled, falling forward until she rested upon him. Her face and lips close to his. Peter rubbed his bottom lip on his teeth. His willpower wasn't going to abate. He could resist the urge. The urge to...

Peter tangled his fingers in Agatha's hair, puckered and pressed his lips tight to hers. His vision blurred. Streaks of color resembling the bouquet he brought flew across his vision field. In amongst the chaotic color-filled eruption, he caught glimpses of Agatha. Her eyes were closed. Her hands clenched his arms. He blinked, hoping to regain some semblance of control when—Agatha's lips parted.

Agatha grasped the first solid thing she found. As soon as she took hold, she knew what she'd done. Touched Peter again. This time firmer and with a determined grip. Leaning on him added to the energy zooming around and through them. This wasn't astral projection sex or dream-loving. This was real. Real, so very real. Her imagination was panting on the sidelines urging her to take the kiss where she'd been daydreaming about. Take things to the next level real time. Let desire and attraction replace lust and flirtation.

She inhaled little by little, pressing her breasts more fully touching Peter. Hip to hip. Nether regions touching. Her hands slid up Peter's arms. Strong, firmly muscular arms. Warm, embracing her here and now. Not some made-up fantasy. Not hazy astral projection with the hope that reality would play out. Reality was unfolding in a very delicious manner. His lips reminded her of sugar cookies topped with multicolored sprinkles. Sweet and yummy. The kind she loved to let melt in her mouth and gradually make their way across each of her tastebuds. She wanted another taste. A deeper taste. Taste his masculine essence. Drink in his male pheromones and let the heady rush of being marked as she marked him envelop her. Envelop both of them.

Agatha parted her lips. She traced the fullness of Peter's top lip with her tongue. Saltiness mixed with the lingering sugar cookie sweetness. Nothing bitter at all. She continued familiarizing herself with Peter's lips, tracing his bottom lip with her tongue. Would Peter permit her a deeper taste? A sip from his inner being? A taste that might slip them over the edge?

Peter slid his hands down her arms, not stopping until he reached her hips. He cupped them firmly, holding her tight to him. He rocked his hips back and forth mimicking where he wanted to go. On his next forward rock, he parted his lips. His tongue meeting hers. Tasting, sipping, seeking more.

Their tongues met in the age-old mating dance their nether regions ached to do. Tasting, sipping, marking each other in ways that were as old as the dawn of time. Peter pressed closer to her. His hands rubbing in small circles around and over her hips. Much more and they'd...

Thunder, followed by lightning flashes, sounded outside the shop. The sky grew dark and rain poured down. Steady, strong rain storm was echoing their energy and passion.

Back-to-back thunder rumbled sounding as if nature, Lupa, the One and Luna were cheering them on. Lighting struck the street right outside the shop. Loud pops and sizzles exploded.

Peter let go. Pulled back and tipped his head back. He was not going to howl. Not yip. His wolf could cool his haunches and behave. Peter rested his forehead against Agatha's. "I'm not going to apologize for something we both wanted."

Agatha nodded. "True."

"You okay to sit?" Peter moved sideways creating space between them. They needed to talk about what happened and how they were going to handle this.

"Yeah," Agatha replied, perching on the desk. "Is this one of those gee that's great let's not do that again moments?"

Peter smiled, combing his hands through his hair lest he thread his fingers into Agatha's hair and fling them back into the pool they'd just stepped out of. "No, it's no mistake. We flirted around it. Tried to deny what was evident. I'm serious about dinner with me at MacGruder's. I'll prepare it. Home-cooked meal. Simple fare as there's not much stock on the shelves yet. Dessert from Mitchell's. Flowers and vase from Staxon's Floral shop."

Agatha rose, chafing her arms. "How do we get across the street in that?"

Peter turned and groaned. He'd chalked the lightning and thunder up to their magic interlacing and igniting reactions. Not nature deluging outside. "Uhm, trash bag rain coast and plastic shopping bag rain hats."

Agatha chortled. "Did that as a kid. One of the best times my younger siblings and I had playing in the rain. Mom told us not to get wet. We didn't for the most part."

"Done that a few times, too." Peter chuckled. "What kid hasn't."

"How are we going to dry off?" Agatha asked as the rain came down harder.

"Got a change of clothes with you? Out in your car?" Peter started down the hall into the back room. "I turned part of the old storage room into a mini apartment complete with a compact washer and dryer. Even a sofa sleeper."

"Are you suggesting I sleep with you over one kiss?" Agatha was already getting trash bags out and handing him a shopping bag.

"Hon, I'm suggesting we have dinner. Dry our clothes while we wear our changes. Pull out the sofa sleeper and binge-watch old movies. Where it goes from there is up to your imagination igniting mine. Cuz it doesn't look like that storm is going to let up anytime soon."

"I'm supposed to ignite your imagination?" Agatha cut arm holes on the sides of two large trash bags. She pulled two more from the dispenser roll. "Aren't you overlooking something?"

"What, you don't have a fertile imagination? You gotta have one to come up with matchmaking nuptials or prenups." Peter took the two trash bags Agatha held out to him. "Most of the matchmakers I've known say creativity is essential to match bonding ceremonies or pair bond weddings."

"I didn't say I don't have an imagination." Agatha cut holes in the top of the two trash bags she held. "I'm standing here making trash bag raincoats with you. I'm being the creative one."

"I've got my rain hat on. Just waiting for you to finish tailoring my raincoat." Peter pointed to his head. He held out the two trash bags Agatha handed him a few minutes prior.

Agatha grabbed the bags, cut holes in the top of each, and tossed the bags back at Peter. "We can make a dash for my car. I can get us over to MacGruder's parking lot. Both our vehicles in the same place."

Peter nodded. "Worth a try. Best dodge and dash tween the raindrops now. That last clap of thunder echoed pretty good."

Agatha stuffed her tote and fanny pack in a plastic shopping bag. "Got the stuff you brought in with you?"

Peter held a large trash bag up. "All in here."

Agatha pointed to the alarm system. "Once I set it, we got two minutes to exit and lock the door from outside. I really don't want to explain another false alarm."

"I understand. Sheriff Knox and Deputy Police Chief Jones are my cousins." Peter moved up to the door.

Agatha heaved a sigh and keyed in the alarm code. Who else was Peter related to? Half of Cauldron Falls? Who else in Sylvan Valley? If this ever got out, she could see the supernatural's version of a shotgun wedding happening. Magic wands and morphed shapeshifters lined up on the sides of the moonlit aisle she and Peter were supposed to walk down. Oh Luna, why did her imagination decide to take that wild turn?

Agatha pulled the door open, tugged her keys out of her jeans pocket, held them up and dashed out the door. She didn't need to look back to see if Peter was right behind her. His hot breath warmed her neck from the moment she'd opened the door.

Peter pulled the door closed with a heavy slam. "Hand me the keys. I'll lock it."

Agatha dropped her keys in his hand. She turned away, muttering. "Crap my car's at the far end of the parking lot."

Peter heard and felt the lock click. "We can make a run for it."

Agatha pointed to the rapidly rising stream running off the building overhang. "Too bad we didn't bring a couple bars of soap. We could have saved time washing us and our clothes at the same time."

Peter snickered, kissed Agatha's cheek and clasped her hand. "On the count of three, we dash. One."

"Two. Three." Agatha called out, letting go of Peter's hand. She stepped forward, knowing that after this afternoon and into the night, her life was changing. Big time changing.

Peter followed Agatha across the parking lot, dodging puddles and fording ankle-deep streams of pooling rain. Third parking space from the end of the lot, a tan SUV beeped and flashed its lights as they got closer. "Your car?" he asked, pausing close to the front of the SUV.

"Yes. Get in. Passenger door's unlocked." Agatha opened the driver's door and scrambled inside. She put her plastic bag in the back on the seat.

Peter paused. A flash of lightning followed by two claps of back-to-back thunder echoed right over him and off the buildings close by. He grabbed the passenger door handle, opened the door and quickly got in. "That was too close for comfort."

Agatha started the engine. "Seatbelt on?"

"Yes."

She put the SUV in gear. "Here we go."

Fifteen minutes later, they pulled into MacGruder's parking lot. Inching through running water, deluging rain, lightning flashes, and dimming outdoor lights, they found a parking space close to MacGruder's back door. Peter patted his jeans, locating his keys. He glanced at Agatha. She gripped the steering wheel. She let go two quick sighs and spoke. "We're here. I hope we got lights and heat."

"Me too. I can improvise meal prep. The wood-burning pizza oven still works. Got wood briquettes for it." Peter opened the passenger door. "Your bag with your other clothes?"

"On the floor behind your seat." Agatha shut the engine off. "Mad dash number two commences now."

Peter grabbed his bag, Agatha's duffle bag off the passenger back seat floor and checked where Agatha was. She stood near the front of the SUV, holding her bag, and held her keys out. Peter closed the passenger side doors and made his way toward Agatha. The SUV's light flashed and the horn sounded.

"Welcome to MacGruder's. Fine dining awaits you." Peter started toward the door with the outdoor light flashing on and off over it.

"I hope your shower works. Rinsing off and dry clothes are our next venue." Agatha dashed toward the door. Would the electricity hold out until they got the door unlocked and got inside?

"I heard the lock click." Peter turned the knob. "I'll get the light inside."

Lights blinked. Thunder rumbled. Lightning flashed.

Silence. Pitch black darkness. Crackles of rain hitting the pavement sounded.

Louder pitter-patters started. Large drops fell. Pitter-patters echoed faster.

Agatha grabbed Peter's hand, thrust her other hand out in front of her and muttered, "Where the frack do we go from here?"

CHAPTER EIGHT

Whispers of the Future

Friday Morning

Agatha rolled over, punched her pillow and sighed. Thursday night. Never in her wildest imagination, dreams and fantasies could she conjure up what happened. Yet, it had. Reality was so much more unique than fiction. Magic aside. Somewhere in her broken spurts of sleep, she dreamt Luna and the One telepathically spoke to her. Invocations and prayers were answered. A simple thank you would do. Agatha pulled the covers higher. She shook her head. Had she stuck her tongue out and blew a raspberry at Luna and the One?

"I must love to live dangerously doing that." Agatha closed her eyes, willing her mind to quit tossing images of Thursday night back up into her closed eyelid vision.

Darkness enveloped them. Peter bumped against her. Soaked, chilled and soggy weren't thrills she'd planned on. Short trot across the parking lot. Into her SUV and across the street to MacGruder's. Mother Nature, Luna, Lupa and the One had their agenda going. Water had reached midway up the tires. Looking for other people fleeing the storm and headlights of other vehicles had consumed her and Peter's attention. Concentration was frazzled and vigilance was on high. Gunning the engine had worked to a point. One she was sure probably had both of them wondering if she was a demolition derby driver in a previous life. Finding a parking space in the diminishing light and darkening parking lot hadn't been easy. She'd parked. They got out of the car and made it inside.

Listening to Peter cuss in old Latin ignited the giggles. She knew why he did that. To keep from saying incantations that shapeshifters weren't supposed to say. A bit of bullshitting supernatural parents and magic parents used to keep their kids from trying magic before they understood their traits and powers. Some shapeshifters had magic abilities due to the mixed heritage many had. Keeping teenagers from turning each other into newts and warted frogs took something that would partly scare them. Peter cussed creatively in English and old Latin as they ventured deeper into the darken interior of MacGruder's.

"When you're done fussing and cussing, I got a question." Agatha tapped her fingers against her leg. The chill of the cooled air from the last blast of the air conditioner rippled over her. Shivers iced their way up and down her wet legs, arms and over her clothes. Drops of water ran down her cheeks and over the trash bags soaking her sneakers and socks even more. By the time she got out of all this, she bet she could fill a couple of five-gallon buckets twice over.

"I'm done. Thought I could conjure a bit of light. Been too long since I did simple magic. My Granny was a hybrid shifter and magic. Taught simple beginner spells." Peter scuffed his foot forward.

"How well do you know the layout?" Agatha wiped water off her face.

Peter laughed. "Like the back of my hand in *broad daylight*. Pitch black, forget it."

"Frack!" Agatha reached out, hoping she connected with Peter. Anything else, and she'd start screaming. "Put your hand out to the side."

Peter gripped her hand. Heat shot into her palm. Agatha gritted her teeth as the heat inched its way over her wrist and dissipated. "Do you have any memories of where a blessed flashlight might be in this section? Like close to the fuse or breaker box?"

"I might if I close my eyes and move forward." Peter let go of her hand.

"Put your hand back where it was. Open your eyes." Agatha sighed. "Describe what you remember, and let's see what we can feel or stumble into."

"Can try it. Don't blame me if you stub your toes and run into something." Peter scuffed his other foot close to her. "If we back up the way we came in, there might be a set of shelves there."

"Okay, backwards we go and don't let go of my hand." Agatha moved two steps backward, carefully listening as they inched their way back toward the door.

Five minutes passed as they scuffed, stepped, and scuffed some more. She reached behind her. Her hand hit cold metal. The back door. Praise Luna, they'd gotten that far. Now what?

"We're at the door." Agatha tightened her grip on Peter's hand. "Your left is my right. Your right is my left. Which way do we go now?"

"To my left, there is a set of shelves maybe three or four high. Let me know when your hand touches them." Peter shuffled forward.

"Got 'em." Agatha clenched the edge of one shelf. "Right or left for where you think a flashlight or something might be?"

"We keep going for another set of shelves, and there is a space between it and the next set. Breaker box is on the wall. I think there's an emergency flashlight lantern on one of the shelves we come to next."

More shuffling and scuffing of feet sounded as they made their way inch by inch, shelf edge by shelf edge, to the space between the set of shelves and the next.

Agatha tugged Peter's hand. "Do you remember if the safety lantern is on the upper shelf or lower?"

Peter stumbled forward. "Ouch."

A rattle sounded close to where Agatha stood. She mumbled a quick prayer and slowly ran her palm over the edge of the shelf onto the cool metal surface and back toward the wall. Two-thirds of the way back, she touched something. She inched her fingers up the object. Buttons. A strap. She pushed one of the buttons, blinked and dropped Peter's hand. Light flooded the small area around them.

Agatha rolled onto her back. Peter turned on his side, snoring softly. After they'd navigated their way through the back office maze and kitchen, they climbed the four steps into the medium-sized storage area, now Peter's makeshift apartment. Shucking wet clothes and trash bags had taken longer than either of them anticipated. Dinner became what each of them could scrounge up from the identifiable canned and dry goods they came across. Bean and bacon soup, with pizza crust roll-ups filled with pepperoni and pizza sauce plus warm seltzer. They'd towel-dried their hair in front of the pizza oven until the briquettes cooled. Wearing one of Peter's t-shirts and her workout leggings plus a pair of his slippers he managed to dig out of a box of clothes he stashed for emergency purposes, had her glad no one could see either of them. Peter wore tie-dyed sweats, a faded slogan t-shirt and an old pair of gym shoes. What a scruffy pair they made.

They'd played a what-if improv storytelling game for entertainment. Argued over what was correct or not in the storyline. Snickered and sighed as they finished a second bottle of wine. Somewhere around midnight, they crawled underneath the blankets and sheets Peter unearthed from another unmarked box and drifted off to sleep.

Agatha tossed the covers off, sat up and shoved her feet into Peter's slippers. She blinked as she pulled back the towel covering the one window of the storage room. Daylight flooded in. Blue sky, not a cloud from what she could see. She rolled her eyes heavenward and stuck her tongue out. Luna, Lupa and the One had gotten them good.

She made her way to the bathroom checking their clothes where they'd draped them on boxes and chairs. Still damp. She had the rest of a change of clothes in her duffle. Drying her sneakers would take time now that they might be able to run the dryer. She could shower and leave. Question was, could she do it without anyone seeing her? What time was it?

Agatha located her fanny pack and duffle bag. She pulled her phone out. Part of her fanny pack was damp where the rain had penetrated the bag she'd hastily stuffed everything into before leaving the shop. Praise Luna, her phone was dry. She turned it on. Low battery light flashed, and the screen lit up. Three missed calls. Four text messages. She scrolled through the various other messages lighting up the screen. Last message cleared. She glanced at the top of the screen—*Eleven A.M.!* She stuffed her phone back in her fanny pack, grabbed her duffle bag and headed toward the small bathroom.

 The medium-sized shower stall took up one side of the corner bathroom. The makeshift door didn't latch unless it was locked. Not something she was going to do after Peter's warning last night. Locking it could mean not getting out until someone picked the lock. The used door came with a faulty lock. Not that he worried about needing to lock the door. She sighed, remembering Peter's other statement about doors and locks. The storage room door latch with a hook and eye from the outside. Inside was a string and nail on the wall. He hadn't gotten around to getting the door replaced. Agatha located the bottle of combination body wash and shampoo in her duffle bag, hastily shucked her clothes, and turned on the shower. Warm water soon replaced the initial blast of cold water. She ducked under the spray, wetting her hair and body. She poured a dollop of body wash in her hand and started washing.

 Peter reached out beside him as he stretched. Nothing. He sat up, rubbed his eyes and looked around. Daylight poured in through the storage room window. He blinked, squinted and glanced around the room. Had Agatha snuck out? Had last night been that dismal? He'd blown another first date?

 He threw the blankets off and sat up. Peter rose ready to go looking for Agatha as he stuffed his feet into his gym shoes. Partway to the window, he paused. Sounds of water running and bits of an off-tune hum reached him. Grinning, he maneuvered his way through the maze of boxes and furniture, around damp clothes draped on boxes and wet bundles of trash bags and plastic shopping bags. He reached the door, grabbed a towel off the box where he'd left them last night, shucked his clothes and shoes, tiptoeing into the bathroom.

Agatha hadn't turned on the overhead light. The low-wattage nightlight illuminated the outline of the shower. Peter knew from buying the shower stall, two people could easily fit. The large lip wouldn't let water overflow. The curtain would wrap around one of them. Nudity hadn't been a problem last night. Disrobing in the dark with the occasional flashlight beam from their phones hadn't been an issue. The beams were directed away from the separate areas they undressed in.

Peter knocked on the sink as he approached the shower. "Mind if I join you?"

Agatha's gasp echoed out of the shower stall. "Would it do me any good if I did?"

"Well, sorta. I could close me eyes and let you get by." Peter grinned at what he expected Agatha's response to be.

"Yeah, and see you buck ass naked." Agatha's sigh broadened Peter's grin.

"There is that. Seriously, we undressed in front of each other last night." Peter took two steps forward.

"We didn't see each other. No ogling happened." Agatha peeked around the shower curtain. There was no mistaking the view middle of the small bathroom. Peter G. Drake, wearing nothing but a cheesy Cheshire cat-like grin, stood holding his hand out.

"I could wash your back and you mine." Peter took hold of the curtain. His fingers touching hers. There was no missing the energy and heat rolling off him and onto her. Desire and want mixed sending their strong pulsating signals over and through her. Did Peter feel them, too?

"We're bound to get to this at some point." Agatha turned the shower head toward the back of the stall. "Come on. Not like we gotta do show and tell."

Peter laughed. "Nope, that is happening now. On its own, too."

Agatha turned sideways and held out the bottle of shampoo body wash mix. "This okay or you one of those gotta have special soap dudes?"

Peter stepped into the shower, pulled the curtain shut and reached for the shower head. "It works great for me. Question is, are you ahead of me in the washing or just starting?"

Agatha turned Peter's hand palm up, squeezed a dollop of body wash in his hand, and put the bottle back on the corner soap dish. "Here's the drill. You wash my back. I wash yours. Each do our fronts. We help each other wash hair."

"Sounds good." Peter stuck his hand under the shower spray. "Last question, are touching other parts allowed?"

Agatha closed her eyes. An image flashed across her mind. A grinning wolf, the moon face laughing and the One winking. Deity magic at work. Ah, well. She and possibly Peter asked. The deities answered. Agatha opened her eyes, turning around as she spoke. "Deliberate roving hands? Not this time. Larger shower and more time, possibly."

Peter stuttered twice. Nothing came out except "I-I."

"Start washing, please. Hot water is gonna run out if we don't." Agatha worked her lathered hands up and down her front.

Peter worked his lather-slicked hands over her shoulders, briskly rubbing strokes down her back and quickly across her buttocks. "I need more wash to do my front and hair. What about your hair?"

"Help yourself. I'm rinsing my front." Agatha ducked under the spray, sluicing water down her torso and guiding it over her mons and pelvis.

Peter brushed against Agatha as he reached for the body wash. Heat slapped at him, leaped onto his arm and spiraled its way lower. Lupa, help him. He had to behave. That was the agreement. He upheld his agreements.

He worked a generous dollop of body wash in his hand and stuck it under the spray. He tapped Agatha's shoulder. She turned partway toward him. "You gonna need this to do my back."

Agatha took the bottle, careful to not touch Peter. She worked body wash into her hand and put the bottle on the soap dish. Peter muttered as he turned his back to her. Agatha pressed her lips together. They were both having I got you moments, behaving as if showering together was an everyday thing. She worked the body wash over Peter's broad shoulders and back. Long strokes from shoulders to the top of his buttocks. She flexed her fingers. Cupping firm male buttocks had been part of her fantasies for some time. Did she give in and cop a feel? Was that going against their agreement?

She inhaled, considered what washing back entailed, and that Peter had washed her buttocks. Agatha nodded, grinned and reached forward with both soapy hands.

Peter straightened. He started to glance at Agatha. Whispers tingled his ears.

You been wanting a woman who understood you. Didn't mind touching you. You gonna complain now that one is doing that?

Peter slipped his tongue between his teeth, hoping he didn't blurt out his response. He looked down at his lathered hands, shrugged and started washing. If evidence of his desire arose, well that was a deal with it in the moment item.

Agatha rewet her hair, worked the lather on her hands through her hair and rinsed. She waited until Peter started to turn around. "I'm done. You got the shower to yourself to finish up."

Peter nodded and moved under the spray as she exited. Agatha toweled off and wrapped her hair in the towel. Evidence of where Peter's thoughts were caused her to grin again. Behaving was something they'd pulled off. Could they continue behaving as they dressed and discussed the rest of the day?

Twenty minutes later, a knock rattled the storage room door. Peter looked up from the couch where he and Agatha sat waiting for her shoes to finish drying along with the rest of their clothes in the dryer. He stood, walked over to the door and unlatched the string off the nail. Outside the door stood Randall, Marjorie and another dude, plus Carlos, Ingrid, and Fran Mitchell.

Peter stepped back. "Something wrong?"

Marjorie opened her mouth and swiftly closed it. She glanced at Agatha who looked up from the magazine she held. Agatha nodded and went back to reading the magazine.

Randall entered the storage room. "Boss, this is none of my business."

"True," Peter replied.

"What is my business is setting up. Getting the roasts done. The rest of the food and who's working tomorrow night." Randall turned to Agatha. "Morning, ma'am. Brunch is available in the kitchen."

"Thank you, Randall." Agatha tossed the magazine on the couch as the dryer buzzed. "Peter and I will be down in a few. Coffee and omelets with a couple of Fran's scones will be great."

Randall nodded and moved past the rest of the group. Fran grinned and left. Carlos and Ingrid shrugged and followed Fran down the steps. Marjorie started up the steps. "You got some explaining to do."

Peter moved in front of Marjorie. "No, we don't. Maybe you have explaining to do about the dude with you."

Agatha walked over to Peter, laid her hand on his shoulder, and said, "Peter, meet Terrence, Marjorie's twenty-full moons match. Terrence, meet Peter."

Terrence shook Peter's hand and clasped Marjorie's arm. "No one has any explaining to do. Except them to each other and what they're gonna do about this."

Terrence and Marjorie exited. Marjorie looked back twice, shaking her head and mumbling.

Peter emptied the dryer, set the basket on the couch, and handed Agatha her shoes. "Sorry that happened."

"Nothing to worry about." Agatha put her sneakers on. "Thanks for drying my clothes. Thanks for a fun evening and night. The shower was fun, too."

Peter tossed his old gym shoes in the open box close to him. He looked down at his sweats. "Think I need to change?"

Agatha chortled. "Probably. You are going into a business brunch setting. Looking the owner part is pretty much expected."

"Okay, meet you all down in the main kitchen in ten minutes." Peter crossed to where the items from their plastic shopping bags set on two boxes. He retrieved the small box he'd hoped to present to Agatha yesterday afternoon. He hastened back to the couch. "Before you go, here's something for you."

Agatha took the box, set it on the couch, and looked up at Peter. The white box, now gray in places thanks to the rain, was tied up with a red and white ribbon. The lettering read Staxon's Floral. Luna help her if Janet Staxon knew what the box held. She and Marjorie were cousins. Very close cousins. Referring business to each other. If Marjorie found out what was in the box—Agatha didn't need more ribbing about Peter. More was sure to come since the 'crew' as Peter kept referring to them had decided she and Peter needed rescuing.

"Go ahead and open it." Peter sat beside Agatha.

"Does Janet Staxon know what's inside?"

"To a point, yes."

Agatha groaned. "How much to a point?"

"Open the box, and I'll explain." Peter tugged part of the ribbon off the box.

Agatha finished taking the ribbon off the box. She tore open the top and reached inside.

Plastic wrap crunched as she lifted each item out. A vase and—Cookies! Fran's bridal shower cookies? Agatha laid the cookies side by side on the couch. Peter couldn't be...could he?

Agatha turned the cookies until she could make out the writing on each. She read the message twice and glanced at Peter, who nodded and burst out laughing. "Now you ask me to go out on a date? Have dinner with you?"

"Since we've had our first date, how about you and me hang out together tomorrow night?" Peter chortled. "By the way, I decorated the cookies. Fran sold them to me. Janet gave me the vase to put the flowers in I gave you yesterday."

"I'll share something with you." Agatha put the cookies and the vase back in the box. "Matchmakers are supposed to be mated or matched. I've been hiding a secret for the last eighteen months."

"Before you spill yours, I'll share mine." Peter took Agatha's hand. "I've avoided getting involved with anyone. Too many broken hearts and mistakes. Match attempts that fell flat."

"This matchmaker is available and unmatched." Agatha gazed at Peter intently.

"Good, 'cause I don't judge a matchmaker by their own success. Their heart is different than their clients." Peter winked and nodded as Agatha spoke.

"Should we go ahead and fool them all tomorrow night?" Agatha kissed Peter's cheek.

"Are you saying yes to our second date?" Peter brushed his lips over Agatha's.

"Sure. We'll get through the night and keep them all guessing. And tight-lipped." Agatha rose. "Now I need coffee and food."

"Me too." Peter grabbed his jeans and ran to the bathroom, adding. "Five minutes to change and find me a shirt, please."

Agatha hunted through the box Peter found his slogan t-shirt in. She held up two shirts. The first she tossed back in the box. The second she tossed to Peter. He read the front of it and laughed. He pulled it on and offered his arm as they exited the storage room.

Let the rumors fly. After all, Peter's shirt said it all. "Love to Keep Em Guessing!!"

CHAPTER NINE

The Dance's Spell Of Love

Saturday Night

Peter leaned against the bar, inhaled and smiled. Spiced wine mulled with bits of pumpkin, nutmeg, cloves and allspice plus a hint of cinnamon brewed on the double hot plate Randall had set up. The tip jar overflowed during the early evening happy hour. Cauldron Falls and Sylvan Valley generously gave to charity. Nashville's animal rescues, food banks and shelters would receive a large anonymous donation early next month. Cauldron Falls and Sylvan Valley's food banks, animal rescues and provisional housing shelters knew who their donors were. No one kept their donations secret. None had to. Community chipped in, took care of who needed it, and didn't expect repayment except for paying forward. Those that were helped, helped others. Something that some places missed.

The kitchen door swung open. Randall exited, pushing a double-tiered cart. Three serving staff were setting up the buffet line. Two others were setting tables with utensils, napkins and condiments.

Setting up that afternoon had been a hoot. Terrance had Marjorie climbing ladders, hanging crepe paper and singing loudly with him as the local radio station played oldie Halloween favorites interspersed with local artists. Orange and red crepe paper hung from the ceiling. Jack-o-lanterns illuminated by battery-operated tea lights lined one end of the bar. The red and silver bowls Siobhan Jones donated mixed well with the dining table's white vases, moonlight lilies, and deep red carnations. A bit of winter, a touch of moonlight and the red of love. Siobhan's other donation, the full moon spotlight, added enough light that the dimmed overhead lights allowed all to see the silver paper stars hanging from the crepe paper in constellation configurations.

Peter chuckled. That had been a Friday night event in itself. Three hours eating, drinking, and challenging each other over what each constellation was and how to hang the stars. Someone had rushed to the library right before it closed and checked out three books on star gazing. First thing on his to-do list on Monday was return the books. His trepidations weren't coming true. Everyone worked together, chipped in, and got things ready to go. The party room doors were opening soon.

Lincoln and his date manned the coat attendant room. A peg board with numbered key rings on it would hold the attendee's car keys. Each peg held two sets of numbered key rings. One for the car keys. The other for the checked coats and jackets. The two teens overseeing parking and valet would earn tips, a hot meal and dessert, plus fifty dollars each for the night's work.

Peter glanced over to where Agatha and Marjorie were setting up their table, close to the patio doors. After Thursday night's rain, everyone agreed that outside activities weren't happening. Somewhere around one a.m., the moon would appear if the clouds dissipated. Peter didn't have any of his fingers or toes crossed over that happening. Pictures of the blue moon captured by the local observatory played across the large screens on either end of the party room. Halloween at its finest was happening. He had a bit of his own magic spell-casting to do.

Peter cupped his hands around the battery tealight candle next to him, closed his eyes and began his incantation.

Light of hope
Light of joy
Hear my heartfelt wish
Reveal to me tonight the one
The one meant for me and me for her

He raised his cupped hands and laid them on his face. He inhaled and exhaled three times, repeating the incantation. He opened his eyes as he lowered his hands. Lupa, Luna and the One had already shown Agatha and him they were meant for each other. Tonight was about believing in the revelation that they'd been shown.

Agatha glanced at her watch. Ten minutes until the doors opened. Ten minutes until Peter could claim her for mingling. She'd spent the better part of the afternoon shopping and getting her hair done. Short hair didn't need much doing. Her stylist had shampooed, conditioned and blow-dried her hair so her natural curls framed her face and curled all over her head. Agatha rubbed her lips together. Peter had commented on her lilac and mauve print skirt and top. The grey sweater she wore accented the colors. Marjorie asked her twice who was she trying to attract. Agatha replied no one. Marjorie left well enough alone. Agatha checked the table again.

Two legal pads sat side by side. One for the males interested in a match. One for the ladies interested in a match. The last ticket count put the RSVPs at seventy-one. Some RSVPs made it known they were looking for quad and triad partners. That meant there possibly would be a few empty slots on each list. Randall would handle the men's list. Those wanting quad or triad partners needed to sign a separate list Randall would have for those.

Marjorie sat in the chair next to her. Terrence volunteered for kitchen duty. He enjoyed cooking and cleaning. Carving the roasts, pulling pans of red au gratin potatoes out of the oven and keeping the butternut squash soup hot along with the vegan and vegetarian salad and pasta dish would keep him busy most of the night. He promised Marjorie a dance or two. Time for dessert and coffee. Agatha smiled as she caught the sparkle of light flashing off Marjorie's hand.

Terrence's proposal had caught Marjorie off guard. Caught her off guard in more ways than Marjorie ever anticipated. Terrence wouldn't let her get off the ladder she stood on hanging the last crepe paper streamers until she said the word yes. Ten minutes of back and forth about why she needed to say this led to bouts of laughter and speculation as to what Marjorie might be agreeing to. Terrence had held up the box as he climbed the ladder up to Marjorie stating she must not want what was in the box. Marjorie's loud yell echoed off the ceiling. Everyone knew she'd said yes. More laughter erupted when Terrence climbed down the ladder walking away, calling out she could come down now. He had other things to do.

Lincoln walked to the center of the party room, clapped his hands and called out. "Doors are opening. Mingling and dinner are happening."

Peter greeted the first few people through the door. He walked outside, rubbing his hands. A chill had settled in the air. The change of seasons was in full swing. Carlos and Ingrid walked up.

"Sorry we're a bit late. Didn't get off work until after six. Shower, shaving and putting this on." Carlos flipped the tie he wore up and down. "Took more time than I liked."

Ingrid nudged Carlos. "You look nice. You tied it right. Just forgot how big your head is."

"Hush, woman. Big heads, big hearts." Carlos leaned over and kissed Ingrid.

Peter tittered. "TMI, you two. TMI!"

Laughter ensued.

"Why you out here?" Ingrid asked.

"Getting a bit of air. Centering." Peter pointed to the small patch of sky where the clouds had parted. "Enjoying the blue moon for a moment. Been a while since I got to see one."

Carlos and Ingrid stood with Peter for several quiet moments, looking up at the night sky and watching the changing scenery as more stars appeared and night settled in.

"Let's get inside where it's warm. Dinner should be served." Peter winked as Carlos got closer. "Plenty of Blue Lagoon Rub and marinade happening."

Carlos grinned, nodding as he and Ingrid entered. Peter lingered, taking one last glance at the sky. His great-grandma told him magic touched those who asked with an open heart and intent. As if Luna and the One knew his unspoken thoughts, the clouds parted, and for a brief moment, a beam of moonlight illuminated him where he stood. Peter gave the moon a thumbs-up and walked inside.

Agatha looked up as three more women added their names to the ladies' list. Randall had reported the men's list was filling up. The triad and quad seekers were about even. A few women had added their names to the triad and quad seekers list.

Marjorie stood and called out, "Last call to add your name to the matches list."

One empty space remained on the list of eligible women seeking full moon matches. A thirty-day commitment to getting to know a potential mate, boyfriend, or friend with benefits, as her cousins called it.

Agatha hoped Peter had added his name to the men's list. She picked up the pen next to the ladies' pad. She turned the pad, glanced down the list, and wrote her name in the last space. She turned the pad back around and faced Marjorie. "Ladies list is full."

Marjorie pushed back from the table. "I'm going to check with Randall on the men's list."

Agatha swiped her sweaty palms on her skirt. Keeping her unmatched status quiet hadn't been easy. Month after month, she'd smiled, helped people match up, and read tarot cards, hoping one spread would reveal a match for her. No luck until Peter G. Drake had arrived. No one had asked who her match was or to see her matchmaking license. Her luck might be changing.

Peter glanced at the list Randall laid on the bar. A numbered line at the bottom of the page had no name. Peter grabbed a pen, printed his name in capital letters in the space and laid the pen next to the pad. He hoped Agatha had done the same. After Thursday night and most of Friday, he wanted the chance to get to know her better. See if what his heart kept whispering to him in his dreams and thoughts matched her heart whispers.

"Okay," Randall called out. "Men's list is full."

"Ladies list is full," Marjorie called out.

"Next ninety minutes are for dining and getting to know the lady who picks you out, gents." Peter came out from behind the bar. "First dance begins in ninety minutes. Good luck, ladies and gents."

Peter walked over to Agatha, holding his hand out. "I'm available if you're interested."

Agatha looked around. Everyone was busy mingling and making their way to the buffet line. She stood. "Very interested. I was supposed to come and tell you that."

"I don't think anyone's going to mind." Peter closed the space between them. He clasped Agatha's hand. Sparks, heat and bursts of color outlined their joined hands. "I claim dinner and the first dance."

Agatha shook her finger at him. "Ladies choice. I'm claiming you. You're impatient."

"Got that right." Peter brushed his lips across Agatha's. "Claimed, marked, and checking out if matching is next."

Agatha grinned. "Dinner first. Dance, then if you are still sure during dessert, we can talk about what needs checking out."

Agatha laid her utensils on her empty plate. Ninety minutes seemed like a long time when she wasn't busy. Dinner's ninety minutes felt like it flew by. She'd learned Peter could cook. The roast, potatoes and soup were delicious. They'd both gone back for seconds. Fran's bread and assorted rolls were awesome. Peter teased he'd stashed a few back for breakfast and made sure the storage room door had the hook and eye on the inside now.

Agatha turned her chair sideways and scooted back until the chair touched the wall. The overhead lights brightened some. A local artist's love song ballad crooned out the stereo's speakers. Peter pointed at her from where he stood close to the bar. He pointed to himself. Made dancing motions and walked toward her. She sipped the last of her water. Wiped her sweaty palms one last time. Her great aunt's insight echoed through her psyche.

Warm heart. Sweaty hands. Warm heart and sweaty hands, listen to your heart. Hear its whispers. Love and pheromones are in the air. Who are you marking, claiming and they you? Watch, listen and know.

Certainly, Thursday and Friday had marked her. Agatha caught herself more than once fanning herself and wondering why her palms were so sweaty. She wasn't ill. Dreaming about Peter and another astral projection love session plus dream sex included penetration this time. Her heart and psyche signaled. Her time to make her interest and possible choice had come.

Peter stood toe to toe with her holding his hand out. "May I have this dance?"

"I want to dance with you." Agatha rose, stepped to the side and faced Peter. "Let the dance begin."

Peter led Agatha onto the dance floor. Couples, quads, and triads moved and swayed their way around and across the dance floor. Peter held his hands up. "I dance with my arms around your waist. Your arms around my shoulders. You?"

"Sounds good to me." Agatha moved so she stood toe-to-toe with Peter. "Do my feet go outside yours or inside?"

Peter chuckled. "Whatever works. I'm an equal opportunity dancer."

His arms around Agatha's waist. Agatha's arms looped around his neck. They slowly began making their way around the small corner space of the dance floor. Reds, blues and greens outlined Agatha with each breath he took. Heat spiraled over and around them with each turn. Sparks shot across his vision field as Agatha tilted her head and pressed her lips to his.

Their lips parted. Tongues met repeating their kiss memories over the last few days. Agatha broke the kiss off, pulling back as the music stopped. Peter slid his hands lower, pulling Agatha tighter to him. "Don't move too far away. Evidence of our kiss, the love sparks and desire are present."

Agatha nodded. "Yeah, spotlight would show on me too." She glanced down at her bust. Peter smiled. "Not a great time to see if the hook and eye on the storage room door work."

Agatha shook her head. "TMI Peter G. Drake!"

"Nah, Just truth. Good old fashioned truth." Peter slid his hands up, stopping when he reached Agatha's waist. "Time for coffee and dessert."

Randall set two steaming mugs on the bar, two dessert plates with pumpkin cheesecake on them topped with fresh whipped cream and a few assorted cookies. "I'll bring ice water over to the table. By the way, Mimi and I are betting on who declares their match first."

"Mimi?" Peter picked up the two mugs. "Keeping secrets?"

"Nope." Randall handed Agatha forks and napkins. He picked up the dessert plates and set them on the table where Agatha and Peter had sat during dinner. "Mimi and I been seeing each other as friends for a while. Time to declare more? Maybe."

Agatha sipped her coffee and set the mug down. "Peter, staring at Randall isn't going to get him to say more. You're not going to egg him into it either."

Peter sighed and sat down. "Dang, I been missing out on things. Wonder why?"

He winked at Agatha and popped a cookie into his mouth.

Agatha ate part of her cheesecake. "Fran outdid it on the cheesecake. Pumpkin pie, a hint of brandy, plus the spices all roll across the taste buds."

"Agree." Peter pushed his bare dessert plate to the middle of the table. He finished his coffee. "Another dance coming up. Shall we?"

"Terrence and Marjorie been manning the table most of the evening." Agatha wiped her mouth and hands with her napkin. "I need to give her a break. Terrence did promise her a dance."

Peter rose. "Our turn to man the table?"

Agatha glanced around the party room. Couples, quads and triads focused on each other. A few same-sex couples stood at the bar looking over the record collections. Marjorie and Terrence rose, making their way toward Peter and her.

"Marjorie and I would like to dance." Terrence held Marjorie's hand.

"Agatha, could you and Peter watch the table while Terrence and I dance?" Marjorie snuggled closer to Terrence.

"I'm fine manning the table." Peter pushed his chair in. "Agatha, you ready?"

Agatha rose. "I'll watch the table. You and Terrence have dessert and coffee when the dance is over."

"Thanks. Terrence and I appreciate it." Marjorie motioned Agatha closer.

"Peter, go ahead. I'll catch up in a moment." Agatha faced Marjorie. "What's up?"

"A few people asked if both of us were matched as you and Peter danced." Marjorie smiled as she continued. "I asked why. A few commented on the aura colors surrounding you. A known shapeshifter said he and his intended could smell your and Peter's pheromones and hormones."

Agatha swallowed, glancing to where Peter sat behind the table chatting with a couple who were late arrivals. Every time she looked at Peter, his aura glowed, flashed mauve, lilac and pulsating shades of red. Love aura colors, for sure. Their love sparks popped and sizzled whether they were holding hands, sleeping, touching each other, or embracing. The love sparks matched the aura colors she saw. Peter had mentioned he saw blues, beiges and patches of white like the white caps of the waves as they rolled onto the beach. She faced Marjorie. "I can say I'm attracted. Getting to know Peter. Matched? I'll let you know."

"Understood." Marjorie followed Terrence onto the dance floor as another slow dance song started.

Agatha made her way to the table. Peter pulled out the chair next to him. Agatha sat down. "Late arrivals okay with a dance and dessert?"

"Yeah. They were declaring their intent at a family dinner. Both their parents insisted there with family present." Peter pulled the match list to him. "Fourth generation founding family on both sides. Keeping traditional ways still a strong thing."

Agatha started crossing names off the singles lists. She tapped the full moon match recording list with her finger. "Can Randall and you adjust the moon spotlight to center on the space in front of the table? People can declare their matches as Marjorie and I record them."

"Sure can. Just need to turn up the brightness." Peter laid his hand on Agatha's. "Got a question."

"Sure. What?" Agatha laid the pen down and looked up.

"You. Me. Moonlight? What do you think?" Peter raised their joined hands and kissed Agatha's knuckles.

Peter tightened his hold on Agatha's hand. She kept staring at him. Had he asked the wrong question?

"Randall and I are going to get the moon spotlight adjusted. We can talk more when I get back." Peter scooted around the table and trotted toward the opposite end of the bar.

Agatha gripped the table edge. Peter's question caught her by surprise. Words failed her as what he said sunk in. She knew what her answer was. Running behind Peter wouldn't work. She needed to get his attention, reassure him at the same time and make her intentions known.

The music stopped as she stood. Randall stood on the same ladder Terrence had used when he proposed to Marjorie. Mimi stood where the moon spotlight would shine once the adjustment was done. Peter steadied the ladder. Agatha walked up to Mimi and whispered something. Mimi nodded, grinned and nodded again. Agatha reached into the pocket of her sweater, pulled something out and pressed it into Mimi's hand. Mimi glanced at her hand, hugged Agatha and moved to the edge where the spotlight shined on the floor.

Peter stood under the spotlight, holding a microphone. "Folks, time has come."

Agatha stepped in front of Peter. She leaned in, speaking. "Yes, time has come. Peter Griffin Drake, you asked me about moonlight a few moments ago. You've unlocked my heart, showing me what it is to believe in connection, attraction, and one more thing."

Agatha dropped to one knee, held her hand up and opened it palm up. A red and white ribbon rested against her palm. She continued speaking, "Peter G. Drake, I'm ready for a moonlit match, are you?"

Peter handed Randall the microphone and knelt next to Agatha. He pulled a small box out of his jeans pocket. "A Brindle Wolf tradition is a full moon match comes with a symbol. The full moon on a silver chain. Until we can get a chain that fits, may I use your ribbon to put this on you?"

"Yes. I accept your full moonlit match proposal." Agatha held out the ribbon. Peter threaded the ribbon through the loop on the full moon charm and loosely knotted the ribbon around Agatha's neck.

Mimi tugged Randall into the spotlight and tied the ribbon she held around Randall's wrist. "Randall, I'm accepting your full moon match proposal."

Randall's mouth dropped open. He moved his mouth. No words came out. Mimi reached up, tangled her hands in his hair, and kissed him.

Other couples lined up close to the match recording table. Marjorie and Terrence were busy recording names.

Peter helped Agatha stand. He slid his arm around her waist. Agatha snuggled closer.

"Thank you," Peter whispered, tipping Agatha's head back. "Thank you for unlocking my heart. Helping me hear its song clearly again."

Agatha reached up and traced Peter's lips with her fingers. "Thank you for finding me. Showing me the beauty of being with someone. Finding someone I want to be their moonlit match with and they mine."

EPILOGUE

Two Months Later

Ralph and Tracey O'Shay, Cauldron Falls and Sylvan Valley's Justice of the Peace and Coven High Priestess, stood close to MacGruder's patio doors. Moonlight poured in through the doors. The prior week's snowfall decorated parts of the patio doors' window panes. Several couples had declared their match choices. Three other couples exchanged marriage vows. Terrence and Marjorie were among them. Peter and Agatha stood near the edge of the bar, waiting.

Ralph and Tracey stepped forward. Ralph spoke first. "There's one last vows exchange happening tonight. When a matchmaker finds her match, it's special. When that match turns into love, a beautiful thing happens. Two people bond together. Their hearts join in relationship. Their lives entwine. Agatha and Peter, please step forward."

Tracey spoke as Peter and Agatha formed the other half of the circle Tracey and Ralph started. "Bonding together is a special moment. A moment when two or more people declare themselves family. The unit of their lives multiplies. Their circle widens. Peter and Agatha, please face each other and join hands forming your first circle together. Repeat your declared vows aloud in front of company and these witnesses."

Peter declared his vows first. "I, Peter Griffin Drake, declare Agatha Marie Clemons is my moonlit match. My heartmate and pair bond. I rejoice that I found you. I love you. Thank you for pair bonding with me."

Agatha declared her vows next. "I, Agatha Marie Clemons, declare and celebrate that Peter Griffin Drake is my moonlit match. My heartmate pair bond. I love you. My heart and I delight that you are part of my world and life."

Ralph and Tracey each held up a two-toned gold and silver ring. They spoke in unison as they handed the rings to Peter and Agatha.

"These rings are symbols of your bonding. Reminders of your moonlit match. May Luna, Lupa and the One bless you forever and always."

Peter slipped the ring on Agatha's finger. Agatha slipped a ring on Peter's finger. They joined hands and held them aloft as cheers sounded.

Luna nudged Lupa and the One, smiling and nodding. They'd successfully added another moonlit match to Cauldron Falls.

Don't miss out!

Visit the website below and you can sign up to receive emails whenever Solara Gordon publishes a new book. There's no charge and no obligation.

https://books2read.com/r/B-A-RAUJ-EQRBF

BOOKS 2 READ

Connecting independent readers to independent writers.

Did you love *Moonlit Match*? Then you should read *A Mate of Their Own*[1] by Solara Gordon!

Cauldron Falls Book #5

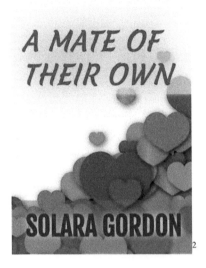

Are a male witch, a wolf shapeshifter, and a non-magical witch ready to move past

their previous failed relationship and be more than friends?

Cauldron Falls' new co-alphas, Daniel McFarmer and his best friend, Kirk Addison,

want Carla Smith as their mate.

Carla knows all too well about not fitting in thanks to her magical family's purist views

on non-magical family members. Letting go of her not-good-enough self-image hasn't

been easy.

---

1. https://books2read.com/u/4E9oJz

2. https://books2read.com/u/4E9oJz

Daniel wonders if he's going to get a second chance at love. Given his failed past

relationships, he's ready for his second-sight magic to fail again.

Kirk doubts anyone finds him desirable. His imperfect shapeshifting and injured leg aren't

getting him many first looks, much less second ones.

When a high school reunion reunites them, can three past lovers embrace their

second chance at love or will old wounds and distrust rip them apart?

Read more at https://solaragordon.com/.

Also by Solara Gordon

Cascade Bay
Love Reborn
Reunited By Choice
Love's Triple Play
Three Hearts In Love
For the Love of Three

Cauldron Falls
Believe In Love
Home for the Holidays
Three Hearts Entwined
A Mate of Their Own
Moonlit Match
A Christmas Reunion

Peyton Corners
Falling for You
Caught by Love's Slow Burn

Standalone
A Heart's Desire
To Love You Again
To Love You Again

Watch for more at https://solaragordon.com/.

About the Author

Solara loves and lives with her partner of 21 years in the Metro DC area. What started out as a bi-coastal romance soon settled on one coast.

A vivid imagination keeps her busy creating her next fascinating romance. She enjoys creating unique characters and watching their journeys unfold. "Love freely given multiplies and will return endlessly" is a key aspect of her stories. Add in alternative lifestyles and her love for the paranormal, and the uncommon becomes the norm in many of her stories.

Her day job in the financial services industry pays the bills while she pens her erotic tales.

Read more at https://solaragordon.com/.